P9-CZV-823

Trapped!

Suddenly the ground and brush around them began to explode with a fresh and furious burst of fire.

"Hell," Alex Nanos muttered as he hugged the ground in the ravine's dense undergrowth. "Cross fire!"

It was time for an act of pure desperation. He signaled for the others to cease the return fire, then yanked two of the M-26 grenades from his web harness and pulled the pins. He rolled onto his back and waited.

"Come and get it, you sons of bitches," he whispered. But he knew that even if the enemy fell for the trick, it would be a close call. Too close, he thought, and gritted his teeth.

SOLDIERS OF BARRABAS

SOLDIERS OF BARRABAS

THE BARRABAS FIX

JACK HILD

A GOLD EAGLE BOOK FROM

W✪RLDWIDE.

TORONTO • NEW YORK • LONDON • PARIS
AMSTERDAM • STOCKHOLM • HAMBURG
ATHENS • MILAN • TOKYO • SYDNEY

First edition November 1988

ISBN 0-373-61627-9

Special thanks and acknowledgment to
William Baetz for his contribution to this work.

Copyright © 1988 by Worldwide Library.
Philippine copyright 1988. Australian copyright 1988.

All rights reserved. Except for use in any review, the
reproduction or utilization of this work in whole or in part
in any form by any electronic, mechanical or other means,
now known or hereafter invented, including xerography,
photocopying and recording, or in any information storage
or retrieval system, is forbidden without the permission
of the publisher, Worldwide Library, 225 Duncan Mill Road,
Don Mills, Ontario, Canada M3B 3K9.

All the characters in this book have no existence outside the
imagination of the author and have no relation whatsoever to
anyone bearing the same name or names. They are not even
distantly inspired by any individual known or unknown to the
author, and all the incidents are pure invention.

® are Trademarks registered in the United States Patent and
Trademark Office and in other countries.

Printed in U.S.A.

1

The orange glow of the setting sun made the waters of Inle Lake dance with fire. This was Burma at twilight, when all the demons and minions of the netherworld came awake and began their nightly prowl. When strange things happened, and all respectable Ung-sa were through with their weaving or leaving the glistening rice paddies to go home with their families and protect their loved ones from the forces of darkness.

But not Pham Hien. Pham had a date with a demoness. He watched the sun begin to sink into the lake, making the lush floating island gardens shimmer and burn, and he pedaled his bicycle with all the fury of a man being chased by hellhounds. Like all the Ung-sa lake dwellers, Pham was highly superstitious, but he was also very poor and greatly in need of money. For that he would brave the things of the Asian nights.

Pham rode his bicycle on the pathway around the southern edge of the lake, up past one of the many weaving villages where "Zimme" silks are produced, then farther north into the hill station of Nam-Hu. He pulled up to the ominous and darkening Paung-Daw-

U Pagoda and parked his bike in front of one of the arched entranceways.

Pham entered the courtyard like a man stepping into an arena with lions. He always hated dealing with the Dragon Lady, but she paid so well for the information. From his farming he couldn't make enough money to take care of Su-Li, his youngest. Su-Li was going blind and needed frequent care in Rangoon's most expensive clinics. Pham couldn't afford that on a regular basis, so he had to start a little business on the side. He became a runner for the many drug gangs and bandit groups from the north. They would pass through from remote places to the north and need messages taken to their contacts in Rangoon. The bandits couldn't enter the city, except on pain of being arrested immediately or executed on sight.

But recently the running chores had not been paying enough to cover the mounting medical bills, and Pham was forced to find another way to obtain cash. He began hiring out to both sides of the street, becoming an informant to a covert group of drug agents who worked on the very fringes of the notorious Golden Triangle region. Pham would be given a message to deliver to the city by a roving bandit patrol or drug caravan. On the night before he made his delivery, he would first take the message to his contact in the drug agency and would be paid twice as much as for his run into Rangoon.

Pham walked into the center of the court and waited. The three sacred Buddhas towered over him, and their serene expressions seemed to promise that Pham would be safe. He was in a sanctuary.

Twilight was quickly becoming darkness. Pham prayed that the lady would hurry and let him go home to his family, where he belonged...away from the frightening shadowlands of crime. He shuddered. He wanted to be home!

Something moved. It seemed to be the shadow cast by one of the Buddhas. Pham squinted against the darkness, looking for his contact. She was already here, waiting for him. Good. She could read the document he carried in the pocket of his work trousers and pay him the usual one hundred kyats, then he could be off. Tomorrow he would deliver the papers to the man at Indochina Exports Limited, and would receive another fifty kyats. He smiled. Life could sometimes be good.

It appeared as though another shadow moved in the more general dimness. It was odd that there should be two of them—the woman always came alone in the past. Pham stopped smiling.

The sun was almost gone. Its rays were holding for one last moment against the night, blazing over the three Buddhas and making them glow like figures of burnished gold.

Suddenly one of the gods spoke to Pham. "Why have you come here?" The god spoke in English.

It must be one of the agents, Pham thought, and felt relieved. "I have brought you the information," he replied.

"What information?" asked the god.

Another shadow moved...and yet another! Pham felt an unnamed dread in his stomach. Counting the talking god, there were five of them surrounding him, behind the Buddhas and in the doorways of the temple.

Pham's hand shook as he gave the talking god the sign of greeting from a Lah opium tribesman, the signal most of the bandits used when greeting an unknown party.

"I have information about a new field of opium to be traded on the markets," he said, hoping to lie his way out of what seemed to be a very bad situation. "There are great profits to be made. I will sell you this information."

"You lie," stated the god.

"No!" Pham said in panic. He was worried. "I know of this . . . I know this to be true. . . ."

Night happened. The shadows detached themselves from the surrounding darkness and became moving figures, clad in black. There were so many involved in the opium wars, Pham thought, that it hardly mattered which of the organizations had set this trap for him. Could be assassins of the Shan State Army or KMT . . . or Karen nationals.

He tried one more time to appease. "I speak the truth. I know where this is! I know—"

"Shut up, you sniveling little fool! Shut your mouth and die like a man!"

"Please . . ." Pham dropped to his knees and began to weep.

The four black creatures moved up and stood over him. One reached down and grabbed his hair, yanked back his head and exposed his neck. Another stood in front of Pham and pulled his ninja from its sheath.

Pham wept silently. Who would look after his family? Who would see to it that his daughter received the medical attention she needed? Su-Li would go blind! He sobbed at the thought, then gurgled as the double-edged knife went in clean and cut left, then right, almost severing his head.

Pham crumpled to the ground, his life draining out of him. His final thought was that he had died while trying to help his beloved daughter. He was a good man. His soul would rest easy.

The killer wiped his knife on Pham's shirt and replaced it in its sheath. The informant had been found and punished.

A tall American dressed in bush fatigues stepped out from behind the god who had talked to Pham. He walked over and looked down at the mess in the dirt, shaking his head. "Check him and see if he has the papers," said the American.

One of the assassins knelt next to the corpse and began searching through the pockets. He found the folded document, stood and handed the proof to the American.

The tall man looked at the papers. "Yep. These are the ones I planted on Ne. This little runt was turning it all over to the DEA." He kicked Pham's body. "Stupid double dealer!"

"Do we take the body?"

"Naw," said the American. "Let some tourists find it in the morning. It'll give them something to talk about when they get back to Toledo."

There was an answering guffaw, and the others chuckled politely. Americans had strange ideas about humor.

IT NEVER RAINED in California. It poured.

The downpour had washed the streets clean of the horde of night dwellers who usually lined up on Hollywood Boulevard. The lone man in a belted trench coat had the whole street to himself. He walked along, his hands in his pockets, his head down, water streaming from his short, almost white hair. He was impervious to the glares of the night people huddling in dark doorways and under shielding awnings, safe from the cleansing rains. They watched the big man walk past as though the sidewalk belonged to him, and they knew that it was best to let him pass. He was coming from a place they didn't want to know about . . . and going to a place where they would never follow.

That night the famous boulevard belonged to Nile Barrabas. He was alone with his thoughts. I don't belong here in Hollywood. I should be bivouacked on some foggy frontier or leading a pack of rat-ass rebels through a South American jungle, not wandering around this dreamland, this place of kids with crushed hopes. . . .

Even the girl hadn't helped his melancholy mood. Her name was Pamela, and she was an actress working temporarily as a cocktail waitress. He had spent a few nights with her, trying to derive some artificial form of relaxation with her. He had left her asleep back at her apartment, and had gone into the wet night, knowing that he wouldn't go back to her.

He had been trying to call Jessup. Lately he'd call Jessup's office every day at two in the afternoon eastern standard time, unless he was already working. Now it had been too long between jobs and Barrabas was getting an unsatisfied feeling. He didn't need the money, because he could afford to retire as a wealthy man. For it wasn't money that kept him going on missions. It was a hunger to be challenged and a desire to live on the edge.

So he'd call Jessup in New York, hoping more with each passing afternoon that something had come in, and only getting disappointment. Jessup was away. His calls were being taken by his assistant, Ducett. Jessup was out of town, in parts unknown.

Barrabas's guess was that he was probably on another of his expansive food binges.

So Barrabas waited and drifted through the neon-lit rains of Hollywood. Actually, he admitted that he needed the time to himself, to be undirected and allow his energies to be recharged and his attention to be focused.

Stopping in front of a little all-night diner, he decided to go inside for a cup of coffee to take the chill out of his bones. He bought a local paper from one of the vending machines in front of the restaurant.

Over coffee, Barrabas scanned the newspaper, looking for a hint of something going down in the world that could mean work for him. He found his fate in two articles on page three.

The first related the President's renewed efforts to win the world-wide war on drugs. More funds were being allocated and agents sent into the fields of battle. A grim determination was evident.

The second, shorter one, told the reader that the U.S. was still obviously losing the war. Another kid had been found dead from an overdose on the streets of Los Angeles's Chinatown. The weary detective assigned to investigate pleaded openly to Washington, "Why don't you people do something? It's not enough to fight this battle on U.S. streets. It's too late here. Plug up the source!"

Barrabas set down the paper and took a sip of his hot brew. A smile was trying to touch his hard features.

He knew.

Jessup would call.

2

To describe Walker Jessup as a rather large individual was like saying there is some sand in the Sahara, yet that was exactly how the senator had described Walker to the agent of the DEA—The United States Drug Enforcement Administration. "You can't miss him," the senator had said with a chuckle. "He's a rather large individual."

The man sitting alone at the designated corner table of the Hilton dining room was huge. He weighed over 350 pounds. He sat at the table, his bulk dwarfing everything else in sight, and glared across the room with a hungry look in his eyes.

The drug agent had to stop and wonder for a moment if this was really the man he had heard so much about, the man known as "the Fixer," who could reputedly put together a covert deal so fast it would make your head spin. The agent, who was beginning to have his doubts, shook his head and proceeded to walk through the dining room toward the big man.

Jessup glanced up at the approaching man and frowned. He looked so typical: gray suit, gray tie on a white shirt, gray eyes. Another shadow executive; a faceless drone working in the back rooms of Washington, sending men out into nameless places on jobs that never really happened. Jessup had been a part of it for so many years that it had become predictable, routine.

The gray man stepped up to Jessup's table. "Mr. Jessup."

Jessup nodded and shook the agent's proffered hand. He didn't stand. Politeness was not one of Jessup's fortes.

The agent sat in the chair next to Jessup, close to the big man, so he could talk softly. "I've been assured that you are the man to handle the problem we have in Indochina."

"Maybe," said Jessup. "What's your name?"

"Call me 'Dean'."

"Ha!" went Jessup, his chins quivering. "Dean from the DEA. That's cute."

"Something like that," said the agent, not finding anything humorous in Jessup's comment. His doubts were getting stronger, but he had been told in no uncertain terms that Jessup could provide the services outside normal channels to take care of the deteriorating situation in Burma. The drug agent didn't like getting into risky deals, but the situation had become desperate.

The senator was a real survivor, not only literally but politically, too. On numerous occasions he took it upon himself to become actively involved in the vast shadow networks of Washington. He dealt mostly in secret operations, covert wars and very special projects. Over the years he had become a primary force in the hidden worlds of covert deals and intelligence warfare. He worked strictly outside the bureaucracy, enforcing no set rules or laws. Because he was known to get the job done, when the drug agent's department needed to put together a "special" project, they contacted the senator.

One of the major factors in most of the senator's secret dealings was this man sitting at the table next to the agent. Walker Jessup was an independent contractor, an ex-CIA operative who knew all the tricks of the trade and used them to become one of the most respected free-lancers in the intelligence community. Known as "the Fixer," Jessup could put together any kind of secret deal. He knew his way into and around the shadowland networks like the back of his hand. When someone in the community was in a bind and had a particularly rough or dirty problem to be solved, they most often contacted Jessup.

The senator had not hesitated in recommending Jessup when the drug agency contacted him about their nasty problem in Indochina. The strong recommendation came with a warning, though—Jessup and his contacts would not be easy to do business with.

A waitress approached the table with a steaming pot of coffee. Neither of the men wanted to order breakfast, so the pleasant young woman poured the coffee and left. She had seen the man in the gray suit in the restaurant before and knew that he didn't like to be disturbed.

The drug agent took a sip of the hot brew and set his cup back on the table. He looked over at Jessup. It was time to get down to business, before the place started filling up with the lunch crowd.

"My agency has a problem," he began.

"So I figured," said Jessup, gulping coffee.

"The President is putting a lot of pressure on everyone in his drug enforcement agencies to take an even more active role in his war against drugs. Everyone who has anything to do with international law enforcement is being asked to lend a hand in this campaign, and that particularly includes us. We have gunboats patroling the Gulf Coast, helicopters flying missions over the southern border, satellites launched for intelligence gathering, and hundreds of undercover officers have infiltrated the enemy around the globe. We are in a real, honest war."

"I'm aware of all that," said Jessup.

The agent continued. "And yet, with all our money and backing and new powers, we are losing a very decisive battle in Indochina. We can't seem to even begin to get a handle on what is going on over there. The conclusion is that we have to take some drastic action. So we called you."

Jessup set down his cup. "Given the nature of your needs, I believe I can help. It will be the usual price, which I'm sure the senator has told you is in the six figure range."

"Yes," said the agent. "He told me."

"Good. I really believe we can make a deal. I'm just the man you need."

The agent took another sip of his coffee. He reflected for a moment and started to look a bit nervous. "Do you think you can get...you know... *them*...?"

Jessup chuckled. All these guys were the same. They didn't like talking about Barrabas and his men. But

Barrabas was a veteran, an ex-Special Forces man, and nobody had been ashamed of him then. And the commandos working with him were all battle-honed warriors who did consider to just whom they sold their services. Yet when these bureaucrats discussed the SOBs—the Soldiers of Barrabas—they all acted as though they were talking about someone throwing up on his new shoes.

Jessup looked at the drug man and just shrugged his massive shoulders. "Sure. Like I said, it's the right kind of job, and for the right price."

The drug agent sighed and looked down at his cooling coffee. He was thinking very deeply about something. After a long moment of reflection, he spoke. "Mr. Jessup, I believe there is something I should tell you before you make a final decision. We did a computer analysis on the odds of success for this mission, and obviously they are very good. But the odds for your man were not very comforting. This will be his fifth mission to Southeast Asia, including his tours in Vietnam, and each time the odds go up against his coming back."

Jessup just smirked at the news. "Do you want me to trust your computers, or do you want me to trust Barrabas?"

The drug agent still wasn't smiling. "I'm afraid **there's more. The specific target is a virtual fortress of** drug dealers and Asian warlords, located far up into northern Burma in the Golden Triangle region. It's the most remote country on Earth. Our own agents have not been able to penetrate this region...at least not go in and get back out again.

"It seems the crime lords and drug barons have formed a type of cartel. For the first time, the opium is being shipped and dealt in this region in an organized manner. The results have been devastating for us. Three times as much heroin is making it onto the streets both here and in Europe. This stuff is strong, top grade, and has already been the direct cause of a number of deaths. Mostly young people. Things like that get a lot of publicity, and the President is not happy."

Jessup nodded sympathetically. "Yeah...I can imagine. It's rough when the boss is pissed."

The agent paused for a moment to finish his cold coffee, then continued. "Burma has long been the site of a very old and continuous drug war with strong political overtones. Besides the heroin that subsidizes the Asian warlords in this cartel, just about every political group, rebel force and private army in the region is into the drug business for the income it provides. In some known instances, heroin has been traded for weapons.

"There are Burmese Communists, Chinese nationalists, Karen nationals, the Shan State Army, KMT, Pathet Lao troops and more...many more," he continued. "They are also at war with one another."

"I know all this, Dean," said Jessup. "It's my business to know this stuff."

"Until now," the agent went on, "we have stayed out of this mess. But the game has changed rules. The heroin is being shipped in massive quantities, in an organized manner, with only mild hitches in Indochina. The President wants this stopped. He wants us to toss a wrench into the gears and halt the machine...plunge the Asian drug business back into a state of chaos."

"And I provide the wrench," stated Jessup.

The Hilton restaurant was beginning to fill up with the late-breakfast and brunch crowd. The two men wouldn't be able to talk much longer.

"You can stop by my office this afternoon and pick up the dossier we have prepared," said the drug agent. "I also have someone you need to meet, an agent from our Asian sector who can provide just about all the specifics your people will require to launch this operation."

"Fine," said Jessup. "I'll be up after lunch."

"There's one more thing I must mention to you." The agent sighed, hesitating again, then looked directly at Jessup. "Your man will be up against one of his own this time."

"What do you mean?"

"An ex-Special Forces captain named Marshall Edmond. He was one of those who remained in Asia after the war to try to make his fortune and to seek adventure in the wilds of Indochina. He is ruthless, according to our profile on him, which will be included in the reports you'll get.

"Edmond has gone to work for the warlord's cartel as their enforcement arm. He has assembled a group of killers and criminals who would make the inmates at San Quentin look like a bunch of nursery schoolers. Edmond and his cutthroats will most likely be direct adversaries to your man and his...fellows."

"Should make things interesting," said Jessup.

The agent stood. He gazed down at Jessup, who remained seated. "I'll be looking for you this afternoon, Mr. Jessup. You know where my office is?"

"No problem."

"Good. I've cleared my agenda until I can completely turn this matter over to you."

"I'll be by your office a little later," said Jessup.

The agent nodded, turned and left the dining room. Jessup remained at the table, pondering the new problem that had been tossed into his lap: a drug cartel of Asian warlords, a mean American expatriate acting as their enforcer...and the Soldiers of Barrabas, to be sent over to clean up the whole mess!

Jessup smiled when he thought about it. Odds or no odds, it was the kind of job Barrabas could really sink his teeth into.

3

Nile Barrabas squirmed in the metal chair, his big muscular frame causing it to creak. Couldn't they have provided more comfortable seats? His eyes started to water and he rubbed them, then focused again to stare at yet another slide being rear-projected onto the screen at the end of the table.

"Colonel Van Minh Tho of the New Mon State Party. His primary objective in dealing heroin is to finance his operations in western Laos and supply his private armed forces with weapons. He has an estate on the eastern border of Burma, on the Laotian front, where he harvests his own poppy fields."

The face being projected on the screen looked like a character out of a Fu Manchu movie. It would have been hard for Barrabas to take some of these warlords seriously if it hadn't been for the fact that he had spent a lot of time fighting wars in Southeast Asia. He had learned to take everything over there seriously.

It was two days after Jessup's initial meeting with the drug enforcement executive. The Fixer had attended the second meeting in the agent's office to collect the file and materials on the project. Then he had returned to his room at the Hilton and called Barrabas in Los Angeles.

Barrabas had been ready, and in short order had booked a flight to Washington. After years spent traveling around the globe, fighting in bush wars as a mercenary, he had developed a special sense for the work. He could almost feel a job that needed to be done. It seemed to coincide with his own inner need.

They were in the basement of one of the main administrative buildings, looking at slides of the men who made up the new drug cartel in Burma. Jessup had given Barrabas the basic details of the mission at the hotel. The ongoing meeting was to familiarize Barrabas with the specific background on the drug business he was to topple.

"Chief Wa Duc, leader of a Wa opium tribe and a ruthless land baron in the far northern and remotest regions of Burma."

The person doing the narration was a respected agent of the DEA who had worked for years in Indochina. Her name was Diana Simone, and Barrabas guessed she was Eurasian. One thing he knew for sure was that she was a looker. Her long, black hair was smooth and shiny, her cheekbones high, her skin had a rich tanned glow, and her eyes were a vivid blue. She was dressed simply in a white blouse and brown skirt, but the drape of the casual loose clothes hinted at a superb figure. She moved with certain grace and fluidity.

"We think the headquarters of the cartel may be located on land owned by Duc," Diana Simone stated. "The bad part is that this includes hundreds of miles of jungle on the northernmost border between Burma and China. Not a very nice place."

"You don't know for sure?" asked Barrabas.

"Unfortunately, no," said the woman, sounding apologetic. "The specifics on the location of the cartel's headquarters was to be delivered to me the night before I left Rangoon for Washington. My informant was uncovered, trapped and murdered. The document he was trying to deliver to me was retrieved by the cartel's killers."

"So where does that put us?"

"Back on square one," said Diana.

Jessup shifted his bulk cautiously in his chair. "I didn't say anything about this one being easy, Nile." He folded his big arms and turned back to the screen. He was really only half watching the slides; he had seen them before. Mostly he was indulging himself in a fantasy about a roast beef sandwich.

Diana pushed the button on her remote control and called up the next slide. She looked across the table at Nile Barrabas. He appeared tired, as if he had been pushing himself too hard for too many years and didn't know when to rest. He reminded her of those burned-out CIA contract agents she saw on occasion, languishing in cheap Asian hotel rooms, men who were totally lost, strung out and filled with deep despair.

She hoped her first impression was wrong. They needed a tough and versatile man to lead the mission. They would inevitably be going into extremely rough country and up against dangerous adversaries. The leader of the strike team had to have a good head when it came to outsmarting men without consciences.

Everyone assured her Nile Barrabas and his men were perfect for the job. But he looked so tired!

Diana watched as Barrabas ran his hand through his short, nearly white hair—a memento of his days in Vietnam. His face looked hard in the glow from the slide projector, his eyes full of dangerous knowledge. She knew some things about this man and his crew of crazed mercs. They called themselves Soldiers of Barrabas, and they had been brought together from dark little corners and strange places for the sole purpose of handling missions like this one.

After Barrabas had spent a number of years as a roving mercenary, a career that had culminated in a South American jail cell, where Barrabas was waiting to be executed, he had been recruited by Jessup to form and lead a team that could get into covert action anywhere in the world and help resolve situations where there was no legal recourse or where it would come too late. Barrabas remained an "unchecked" force, very independent, but it was a known fact that when the going got tough, the secret departments could call on the very best in the business . . . and that was Barrabas.

The next slide came up. Nile Barrabas stared at it for a moment, leaned forward in his chair, and took a sudden interest in the lady's program.

"I think I know this guy."

But Barrabas couldn't place him. He was an American, sandy hair under his ranger hat, big, deeply tanned from many hours spent under the tropical sun, wearing an OD green, Army-issue T-shirt.

Diana let Barrabas study the slide for a moment before she spoke. "Marshall W. Edmond. Ex-Special Forces captain assigned to Operation Griffin with the Intelligence Office in Saigon from 1974 to 1975. It's fairly certain your paths have crossed."

"Yeah... Marsh Edmond...," Barrabas sat back in his chair. It was Captain Marsh Edmond. The hair was a bit longer, there were a few more scars, and he looked older, as if he had grown tired of the games. He reminded Barrabas of himself. "Our paths have crossed."

"Well, they're about to cross again," said Jessup.

"Marshall Edmond is now an expatriate living in Indochina," said Diana. "He has a criminal record as long as the equator. He's been into everything from slave trading in Bangkok to piracy on the China Sea. His current occupation is that of enforcer for the new cartel. Edmond commands a virtual army of killers, drug smugglers and Lah bandits. He's known to be a fierce and ruthless man... and highly dangerous."

It sounded to Barrabas as though Edmond hadn't changed much over the years.

Barrabas had met Marsh Edmond while stationed with MAC in Saigon. There had been something about the ambitious captain that had struck Barrabas as odd right from the first little job they did together. Edmond had fit in well with Liaison in Saigon, being the typically useless bureaucrat, but he seemed to be doing other things, as well. He was always a busy man, not just an ordinary paper shuffler and memo rewriter taking up good space and air in the intelligence offices. Edmond had seemed different.

Barrabas had taken it upon himself to do a fairly low-key investigation that readily revealed that Edmond was indeed doing other "things." He was actually running his own small, private crime syndicate out of intelligence offices in Saigon. Smuggling, black-marketeering and dealing in stolen arms with bandits were all part of Edmond's entrepreneurship.

What really annoyed Barrabas was that Edmond was using embassy connections and U.S. money to back his operations.

Barrabas launched his own campaign against Edmond. He dug through files, made copies of records and put together a good case against the Special Forces captain. When more than enough evidence for a conviction had been compiled, Barrabas went after Edmond.

Edmond knew his game was over. Informants had told him Barrabas was on a crusade to put him out of business, and accordingly, Edmond made plans for his escape.

Accompanied by two MPs, Barrabas went over to Edmond's apartment with a warrant for his arrest. But the posh little suite was empty. Edmond had made good his escape.

The trail was still fresh though. Barrabas went after the captain in the teeming streets of Saigon, but his chase was called short when the larger problems dwarfed the conflict between the two soldiers. The city was under relentless siege, and Barrabas was forced to turn to more important matters that led to his tragic flight from the Southeast Asian maelstrom.

Edmond escaped into the dark underground worlds of Indochina. Like his adversary Barrabas, who had become a mercenary and covert soldier, Marsh Edmond followed the strange life path of the soldier of fortune. But Edmond remained on the opposite side of that fine line dividing the worlds of the two men. Edmond became a pirate, treasure hunter and desperado. His life of crime culminated in his becoming an enforcer for the drug traders. Now he was about to cross paths with Nile Barrabas once again.

"Yeah, this one is ruthless," said Barrabas, still staring at the slide of Edmond. It was all coming back...those godawful days at the end of the war...Saigon...and Edmond! He had been small stuff, something to keep Barrabas busy while the bureaucrats fumbled around, giving up the war. But Barrabas didn't like leaving any job unfinished, and it looked as if he was going to get his chance to settle the score with Captain Marshall Edmond.

"This will be the man the cartel most likely sends to stop you once they discover you've arrived in Burma," Diana said. "Which probably won't be very long. The crime organization has a very active and accurate intelligence network."

"Good," said Barrabas.

Diana Simone thought that a rather strange remark, but it seemed to fit the man Barrabas, who seemed rather like a puzzle to her.

The slide of Edmond was the last of the program. Diana turned off the projector and walked over to switch on the lights. The basement conference room was suddenly lit by eye-watering neon. Jessup and Barrabas both got up to stretch.

Diana looked over at Jessup, hoping he would carry the ball from that point. He must have read her mind, because he started to speak directly to Barrabas.

But he never had a chance to continue. Barrabas was facing them, and he cut into the Fixer's words decisively. "I will accompany Miss Simone back to Burma. From Rangoon I will launch a search-and-destroy mission into the north country, the Golden Triangle region. The objective is to find the warlords' stronghold that is the headquarters for their drug operations and crime cartel. This organization is to be put out of business. Is that the gist of the mission?"

Jessup nodded mutely, and Barrabas walked over to the refreshment table and poured himself another cup of bad coffee from the cooling pot.

"You will most likely encounter Marshall Edmond and his assassins," Jessup warned. "No doubt the man will be fueled by feelings of personal revenge." Jessup hesitated, wondering if he should warn Barrabas of the odds of staying alive on a mission in that part of the world. Deciding against it, the fat man merely added another caution. "Your staying objective and coolheaded, though, will be an advantage in emerging relatively unscathed."

"When do we leave?" asked Barrabas.

"In three days. That should be long enough to assemble the team, and for me to supply your needs. We'll work out all the particulars of your gear. Miss Simone can make the preparations for your arrival in Rangoon. We'll book passage for all of you."

Diana listened to Jessup and winced. He sounded so mechanically morbid. Quite possibly he was sending this man and his team to their deaths. Yet the Fixer just spewed out his frightening little spiel, and Barrabas only stood there and nodded, perfectly content to be going into warfare for money.

She would never understand mercenaries.

4

The 747 swooped over the Asiatic metropolis of Rangoon and angled down for its approach to the runway. Diana Simone watched out the window from her seat in first class and felt mixed emotions about her return. She had been working undercover in Indochina for six long years, but there was still something very fascinating about this land of her ancestry.

Barrabas had learned a bit about the DEA agent's personal background on their long flight from Washington. Her mother was Asian, born and raised in a village in southern Burma. Her father was a member of the famed Flying Tigers in World War II, who stayed on after the war to make a life in Rangoon. He ran an export business for a few years, got caught up in the dark side of the business and was murdered by his unscrupulous competition.

He had left enough cash and business assets to his wife to allow her to emigrate to America and raise their little daughter in style. Diana had grown up in Orlando, Florida, living well and going to the finest schools.

Seeing the constant troubles caused by students using drugs and the grief this brought to the community as a whole, Diana had decided to go into the

DEA. She joined the training program after graduating from college, and within two years she was assigned duty in Rangoon. Her choice of career got her reacquainted with the land of her birth.

The plane landed, and they made their way into the airport terminal. There was a lot more activity around the arrival and departure gates than Barrabas had expected. The government of Burma was not encouraging tourism because of all the minor insurgencies and rebel uprisings. Burma had become a port for only the truly adventurous.

Customs and formalities were usually very slow and tedious at Rangoon Airport, but thanks to Diana's influence and the Fixer's dealings, the two were able to wave aside most of the red tape and move right through. They quickly retrieved their bags and went outside to catch a taxi to their hotel.

Leaving the air-conditioning of the terminal and entering the hot, thick air of the Indochinese climate was a shock to their systems. It was like getting slapped in the face with hot, dirty washcloths. Still, both Barrabas and the agent had had plenty of experience in that department, and it didn't knock them for a loop, as it did to most of those arriving from America.

The taxi took them through the bustling afternoon streets of Rangoon, which generally reminded visitors more of a European or American metropolis than an Asian port. The city had a multitude of flourishing businesses, high-rise office buildings, modern cinemas and nightclubs, hosts of Japanese-made au-

tos, taxis and buses, and hundreds of westernized
stores and shops.

Once outside the boundaries of the city, though, it
became a different world. This was the land of the old
Asia; the realm of pagodas, little villages, jungle and
mountains and a life-style that was definitely un-
Western.

The taxi brought them to the front of the hotel. The
Strand was government run, with plush facilities and
more than one hundred rooms. Besides the usual accommodations, along with a choice of dining experi-
ences, the Strand provided services such as money
changing, arranging excursions outside of town and
supplying guides. It was a good place for Barrabas to
begin organizing his mission into the north.

The porters came to take his bags while Barrabas
went over to the front desk to check in. The huge
lobby was as busy as a New York hotel during con-
vention season. This was also a mild surprise to Barrabas. He had really expected Rangoon to be much
quieter, more laid-back.

After checking in, Barrabas and Diana went up to
his room on the fourth floor. The Fixer had provided
him with the best, everything he needed to make his
mission a success, including a bottle of Cutty Sark
Scotch. The merc had the porter leave his bags, and he
tipped him fairly well. The young Burmese left with a
satisfied grin and Barrabas went into the bathroom to
get a couple of glasses and ice. Diana adjusted the air-
conditioning, admitting to herself that her discom-
fort was a sure sign that she had become too westernized again after her brief visit to the States.

Barrabas poured two drinks and handed one to Diana. He took a long swig of the whiskey. "Umm, good."

"You're a real conversationalist, you know that, Nile?" The lady agent took a sip of her drink, looking at him over the edge of her glass.

Barrabas took another swallow, then walked over to grab one of his bags. He tossed it onto the bed and began unlocking its three safety locks. "You're going to get those files from your office for me," he said. It was a command.

"First I'm going over to my apartment and get cleaned up. Settle in a bit. Then I'll go over to the Embassy and make my report. After that I'll obtain the files on the drug cartel and bring them back here for you to review."

"Okay," said Barrabas, pulling a bush jacket out of the bag and setting it on a chair. "The SOBs will be arriving from their various destinations this afternoon."

"Do you really call them that?" asked Diana.

"What?"

"You know. SOBs. It doesn't sound very nice."

"Believe me...the name fits," said Barrabas. "They don't care what I call them, as long as I call them."

"They sound like a nice bunch of guys," said Diana.

"No," said Barrabas. "But they'll be here in a little while. We have a rendezvous at nineteen hundred hours downstairs in the bar for supper. I want you there for sure, in case I'm not back, so you can start briefing them. They start getting nervous and mean if they're kept in the dark about a mission too long.''

"I'll be there," said Diana.

"Good. I'll give you brief descriptions of the men so you can identify them."

Diana chuckled. "I really don't think that will be necessary, Nile. I have a feeling I won't have much trouble recognizing your men. But you said you might not be back. Where are you going?''

"To test the air," Barrabas answered curtly, pulling his Browning HP in its shoulder rig out of the bag.

"Oh, right! You almost sound like Barrabas the tourist. Why do I have the feeling you're going out to look for trouble?''

"Maybe because that's why you brought me over here," said Barrabas, strapping on his gear. He picked up his jacket and shrugged into it.

"You don't waste any time, do you."

"Time is money," said Barrabas. He reached for his room key and put it in one of the pockets of the bush jacket.

Diana sighed. She didn't have a reasonable argument for him, so she just kept silent and shook her head.

Barrabas swallowed the rest of his drink. Chewing on an ice cube, he looked at the girl agent and gave her his best smile. It wasn't much.

"I'll see you at supper," he said, then turned and walked out the door.

"Don't get yourself killed, sweetie," Diana replied in mock sugary tones, but he didn't hear. He was already halfway down the hall.

AFTER STOPPING BY the money changer's desk and trading his dollars for Burmese kyats, Barrabas headed out into the streets of Rangoon.

The climate, the sounds and the smells all brought back a flood of memories to him as he strolled through the bustling town. His work had brought him to Asia many times in the past, to say nothing of all the years he'd spent in Vietnam with Special Forces. He had fought many a battle in the Indochinese jungles, as well as in the reeky slums of the world's most mysterious cities. There was something about being in this part of the world that made him feel right...whole as the man he was supposed to be. It was almost like being home.

Barrabas strolled along Strand Road for a while, east by the Rangoon River. Then he headed a block north to Merchant Street and continued east into the seamy part of the city.

He walked along Merchant Street, past the roving prostitutes, past the bars and strip clubs. Even in midafternoon these establishments were hopping. The district was like the waterfront areas in every city on Earth—a haven for all sorts of illegal activities. And Southeast Asian cities seemed to be the worst. They attracted a particularly sordid breed of nasties. Pirates, smugglers, thieves, slave dealers and other forms of lowlife gathered and festered in the bars and cheap hotels on Merchant Street. It was not the place to take a date on Saturday night.

Barrabas found the establishment he was looking for—Dragon Eddy's Bar and Grill. The place had a dark reputation that spread throughout the underworld. Any service or deed that needed performing and was against a lot of laws was easy to obtain at Dragon Eddy's.

Barrabas went through the open doorway into the dank, smoke-filled interior. He had to stand still for a moment and allow his eyes to adjust to the darkness and smoke. Then he walked through to the rear of the place. The rowdy patrons didn't pay much attention to him as he moved among them with calm assurance.

He backtracked casually and approached the bar. The bartender noticed him, gave him a dirty look and continued wiping a glass with a filthy bar rag.

"Could I get some service?" Barrabas asked, being his usual polite self.

"English...okay," said the bartender. "I speak it. How I get for you?"

"I'm looking for some information," said Barrabas.

"I get you a drink."

"No, thanks." Barrabas suppressed a shudder. "I need you to tell me something."

"I get you a drink."

Barrabas gave in. "Okay. Scotch. Try to put it in a clean glass."

The bartender ignored him. He served Barrabas something very brown in a dirty glass. No ice. "Fifty pyas," he said.

Barrabas paid him, but didn't touch the poor excuse for a drink that sat there on the bar. He focused on his real reason for being there and tackled the bartender again. "I want to know where Eddy is."

The bartender shrugged and tried to amble away, but Barrabas grabbed him. He just reached over the counter and took the bartender by the back of the head, then spun him around to look into his eyes. The bartender didn't like what he saw there, so he decided to be helpful. He started by trying to smile.

"Where's Eddy?" asked Barrabas, politeness no longer in his tone.

"He in back," said the bartender, filled with a new spirit of helpfulness. "He in back. You let go, and I go get him."

Barrabas let go, and the bartender rushed through a door behind the bar. Barrabas had to wait only a moment before he came rushing back. "He coming. Eddy coming."

"Good," said Barrabas. "And for your trouble you can have this drink."

The bartender grinned. "Thank you, mister." Grabbing the glass, he downed the contents in one gulp, then grinned again and went back to his chores.

A tall, slim man came through the door behind the bar. He was a westerner, but his skin was very white for a man living in this part of the world, a testament to how much time he spent in darkened barrooms. When he spoke it was with a strong British accent.

"Nile Barrabas! If it isn't himself!"

"Hello, Eddy."

"If I said I was charmed, I would be lying," said the bar owner. "I heard you were dead."

Barrabas shrugged. "Just wishful thinking on somebody's part."

"Yes. That's too bad," said Eddy. "So, what brings you into my little establishment? Are you looking for work again? I thought you'd given up that business. You've been gone for some time."

"I'm still around," said Barrabas. "I need to know where the rock houses are located in town."

"Mercy! Why do you need to know that? You haven't developed a habit—"

"A friend of mine has. I'm looking for him. It's important I find him."

"I see," said Eddy, rubbing the back of his neck. "Well . . . it'll cost you for that."

Barrabas pulled a wad of money out of his bush jacket. Eddy stared at it and smiled.

"Well, yes . . . yes. Peel about four hundred Ks' worth off that roll, and I'll write an address down on this piece of paper back here. Then we can trade."

Barrabas did as the bar owner said and got the paper. He didn't bother thanking Eddy. Just turned and walked out.

"Nice seeing you again, Nile!" Eddy watched him go, then decided he'd better tell a few people that Barrabas was nosing around.

The address Eddy gave Barrabas was on Bogyoke Street, in the old industrial district. Most of the buildings were empty warehouses and storage dumps. A few of the deserted places had squatters living in them. Two old hotels at the end of the street had been turned into rock houses and opium dens.

Barrabas stood in the long, afternoon shadow of a warehouse and conducted his surveillance. Junkies came and went, a sad looking group of individuals.

Guards were posted at the doors to each establishment, all heavily armed with AK-47s and various side arms. The insides of the two drug houses were dim, lit only by the haze of weak lamps. Every once in a while Barrabas could see the flicker of a burner as drugs were cooked for use.

He watched for a long while, getting the layout of the front entrances and room arrangements. Then he began conducting his perimeter surveillance, making his way around the two buildings, checking the sides and the back. The grounds were pretty barren, just littered with a lot of garbage and one old Toyota behind the first hotel. There wasn't a lot of cover close to the buildings. Any type of penetration would have to be direct.

Every so often, men who were obviously armed would go through a back entrance to the buildings, obviously to conduct business. These would be the dealers, suppliers and distributors. Barrabas had in mind that chatting with a few of these fellows would be a good idea.

He spent a long time mapping the terrain in his mind, memorizing the routines of the guards and security patrols, checking out the various exits, and he began forming an assault plan. He would share his intel with his men and work out the rest of the details with them.

Thinking of his men made him realize they should be arriving by now. Barrabas had lost track of time while preoccupied with his work. The rendezvous in the hotel nightclub was less than an hour away. He had to wrap things up here and get back to the Strand.

He turned to leave through the alley that connected with Anawrahta Road, and came face to face with two men. They were grinning at him and moving cautiously forward with an obvious purpose.

That was proven when the one on the left spoke. "Ah, Mr. Niles Barramas! We have been looking for you."

They kept moving closer, but slowly, as if waiting for something. The talkative one seemed to spot something, and he nodded.

"We have you trapped now," he said.

Barrabas half turned and looked behind him. Two more thugs were coming into the alley from the Bogyoke Street side. There were two in front of him and two in back. Which was par for the course. The two behind were armed with AK-47s.

With a smile Barrabas turned back to face the thug who had done the talking.

The talker appeared confused for a moment. A smile on Barrabas's hard features didn't look natural. Then the man smiled back at Barrabas—and gave his comrades the signal to attack.

Barrabas reacted instantly. His right hand shot inside his bush jacket and pulled out the Browning. He spun around and in quick succession dispatched shots at the men with kalashnikovs.

The thugs had been running forward but were solidly stopped by the slugs and dropped into the filth in the alley.

Barrabas spun again and blocked the kicks of the attacker in front of him with his left arm. The man evidently knew Chinese Kenpo. That was all right.

Barrabas was an expert in martial arts from around the world.

He took the first kick in the shoulder and the second a bit lower in the triceps. His left arm went numb, but he still managed to use it in an upward blocking motion that caught the martial artist under his heel. Barrabas pushed the thug up and off balance, knocking him to the ground. The killer tried to kick up, aiming at Barrabas's groin, but the seasoned soldier brought the Browning around and shot the thug in the face.

That left one...the talker. Barrabas wanted him alive to try to get some information from him. But the Burmese thug was closing in, and he was mad. He made a straight jab that successfully connected with Barrabas's mouth. The lower lip split and began gushing blood. Barrabas took a step back, momentarily dazed by the sharp pain. The killer struck with his fist and knocked the Browning out of Barrabas's grasp.

Barrabas ducked a blow to the head. He came forward, grabbed the thug by the shirt and brought his knee up in a vicious thrust between the opponent's legs.

The killer was halfway into his next swing when the impact hit him. He heaved and fell forward, gasping. He rolled in the filthy alley, overcome by pain.

Barrabas wiped the blood from his chin with the back of his left hand, then stuck the Browning back under his jacket. He let the man get his breath back before reaching down and yanking on his hair. Pulling the man's head back and his face up, he looked right into his eyes with the unmistakable expression that his life meant less than nothing.

"Who do you work for?"

The thug grunted. "General Than Hyut Linh."

The name didn't mean anything to Barrabas. "Who is he?"

"With Karen Unity Forces." Some yellow stuff dribbled down the killer's quivering chin. "In Burma...not Thailand," he added, as if that explained something.

"Why did the general send you here to kill me?"

"Because you snooping around in his business. You down here in a lot of people's business. There be more!"

"I'll bet," said Barrabas, smiling again. He gave the thug's hair another yank to emphasize what he was about to say, causing the Burmese killer to cry out. "You tell the general that Nile Barrabas is not about to go away. I have a job to do."

"You look for work?"

"I'm going to make work," said Barrabas, still smiling. "With or without the general's cooperation. And that goes for all the others like him!"

Barrabas let the man up. "Now get out of here before I change my mind." Barrabas barely glanced at the thug, who had no doubts he had just cheated death. He decided to move before his luck ran out. He turned and scurried away down the alley like a rat dashing for the nearest cover.

Word would now spread throughout the Rangoon underworld that Barrabas was back in Indochina, looking for trouble. He was setting himself up. It shouldn't be too long before Marshall Edmond and his pack of killers came looking for him. Sometimes the hunter has to become the hunted.

5

The Burmese waiter knew that the three men sitting at his back table would spell trouble. His afternoon shift was over, but he had agreed to stay on to help with the dinner rush and make a few more kyats. Now he wished he'd been less greedy and gone home to his wife.

He had been working at the Strand for almost a month. It was a welcome change from his previous job in a bar on Merchant Street, where the clientele was of a seamy sort. The Strand was pure class. The tips were enough for him and his wife to live on, and the regular salary the hotel paid was like a bonus. He was saving up to buy a car. Life was really going smoothly. Now it looked as if there was going to be a hitch in it.

The waiter shrugged and decided it was just best to do his job. He carried the tray of drinks through the crowded dining room to the corner table where the three men sat, all of them with their backs to the wall.

As the waiter drew up to the table, the one sitting to the right didn't even wait to have his whiskey placed in front of him. He stood and grabbed the drink off the tray. "It's about time! A fellow could die of thirst around here waiting to be served."

The man remained standing as he toasted his comrades. "Here's to swimmin' with bowlegged women!" He tossed the drink down neat and set the empty glass on the waiter's tray. "I'll have another." He had a shock of red hair, and to those in the know, he sounded Irish.

The man in the middle, a big, black American, spoke. "No, you won't, O'Toole. The colonel wants you sober. We're going out tonight."

The waiter served the other two drinks, first setting a double Scotch in front of the man on his left. This one looked mad about something.

He suddenly pointed across the dining room. "What the hell is a good-looking woman like that doing with such a stupid looking ape?"

"Dammit, Nanos!" said the black man, looking even more perplexed. "I don't want you getting into a fight. Save it for the job the colonel has lined up."

The waiter set the last drink on the table and turned to leave, relieved to have done with serving this particular group when he had a sinking feeling. Someone else was approaching!

William Starfoot II pushed through the dining room patrons, totally unconcerned that he might be acting rudely. "My red ass in the morning!" the American Indian called out to his friends. "They'll let anybody in this place!"

"Shut up and sit down, Billy," commanded Claude Hayes. "You're drawing attention."

Billy Two sat next to Liam O'Toole, turning his chair so his back would also be against the wall. He slapped O'Toole's knee. "How you doin', Liam? Staying sober?"

"'Tis a treat to see you, Billy...as usual," said O'Toole sarcastically.

Billy Two just laughed. The nervous waiter asked him if he wanted a drink, and he ordered a whiskey on the rocks. The waiter gave a little nod and darted away.

"I still don't like the looks of that guy over there," stated Alex Nanos, the Greek member of the SOBs.

Hayes rubbed his black brow as if trying to massage away a bad headache. He decided to ignore Nanos. The big Greek was getting impatient from the long period between jobs, and anything Hayes said would probably only make matters worse.

He spoke to Billy Two. "Did you talk with the colonel?"

"Yeah. He's in his room, getting cleaned up. He's already been in a scrap."

"That's more like it!" said Nanos, grinning across the table at Billy.

"He'll be down to join us in a few minutes," Billy Two continued, returning Nanos's smile. "He wants us to stay out of trouble. We evidently have some work to do tonight."

Hayes shook his head and frowned. "That's easier said than done. I just hope the colonel gets here soon."

"I'm here."

The four men sitting at the corner table were all pros. They had fought in war arenas around the world. Their cunning and skill were legendary in the strange vortex of the hired soldier, and they had honestly earned those reputations. Yet not one of them had heard or even sensed Barrabas approaching their table from a side entrance.

"Colonel!" Claude Hayes stood from behind the table to greet their leader. He looked down at Billy Two. "Get the colonel a chair."

Billy Two started to get up but Barrabas motioned him to stay put. "Never mind. We're not staying. We have work and I want to take advantage of the dark as much as possible." Barrabas's eyes quickly scanned the dining room. "Where is Miss Simone?"

"She isn't here yet, Colonel," said Hayes. "At least, no one fitting her description has showed up yet." Hayes was sounding nervous. "I really wish you wouldn't sneak up on us like that, Colonel."

Barrabas's deep-set eyes were normally as cold as ice, but now they were flashing anger. The four SOBs at the table were all glad they weren't in Diana Simone's shoes. Their boss wasn't happy. He was a man who demanded promptness, especially in the field. Rendezvous time was nineteen hundred hours. It was now five minutes after. The female DEA agent was late.

Barrabas was still standing, towering over the four men at the table. All their kidding and playful fighting was over. They remained silent, waiting for orders.

Barrabas didn't need the girl, but he wanted her report. He liked to get all the background and intel in order before becoming involved in the real meat of a mission. When the shooting started, it was too late to start sweating over some neglected details. You went in prepared, or you quickly became dead.

The Burmese waiter returned with Billy's drink. He groaned softly when he saw yet another one at the table. And this one looked even worse than the others, if that was possible. He was still standing, tall and rugged, with coarse white hair and dark, mean eyes that contrasted with the hair. He would even have given the cutthroats on Merchant Street a shiver down the spine. The waiter concluded that the gods were certainly not being fair to him this long evening!

He set down the drink with a trembling hand, trying not to spill it, then turned his attention to the new man. He avoided looking into Barrabas's eyes. "Can I get you something, sir?"

"No," said Barrabas. "We won't be staying."

The waiter breathed a heartfelt sigh of relief. He pretended to smile and had turned to leave, when he saw a young woman heading toward them.

"Well," said Diana Simone, approaching the table. "The merry band gathers."

Barrabas watched her saunter up. "Did you bring the report?"

"Well, hello to you, too," said Diana, her tone full of sarcasm. "You're such a warm and friendly man, Nile."

Diana surveyed the little band of mercenaries. Somehow she just wasn't prepared for this. They looked even worse than she'd imagined. It wasn't just that they looked rough and disreputable. What bothered her was something in their manner that indicated a certain lack of respect.

She felt particularly uneasy about the man on the left. He must be Alex Nanos, the sailor. He was staring at her chest, grinning from ear to ear.

She turned her attention back to Barrabas. He was just standing next to her, glaring. "Aren't you going to get me a chair, Nile?"

Barrabas didn't move. Nanos quickly jumped up and took a chair from the table next to theirs. It had belonged to a female patron who had just gone to the powder room. Her husband was about to say something about the man's rudeness, but when he took in the group at the table next to his, he wisely decided that his wife could stand.

Diana felt bad about taking the woman's seat, but she also didn't want to irritate Nanos. She thanked him politely and sat down.

"Colonel!" said Nanos, still grinning at Diana, "you didn't tell us she was such a looker."

The waiter was still standing by the table. When the lady was seated he asked if he could get her a drink.

"Yes. I'd like to see your wine list, and a menu." Diana had been carrying a briefcase under her left arm. She shrugged the strap from her shoulder and set the case on the floor next to her chair.

Barrabas hadn't budged an inch. "I'll take the report, please."

Diana glanced up at him and attempted to look pleasant. "Why don't we have dinner first, Nile? We can talk business and review the files I brought afterward."

"We don't have time for that."

"Good Lord, Barrabas!" said Diana, her patience gone now. "What do you mean, we don't have time? Time for dinner? I'm starved!"

"You're late," said Barrabas.

"Well, excuse me! I was detained at my office. I've been away for nearly a month, and I have a million things to catch up on. I got over here as soon as I could."

"Let me have the files," said Barrabas. "Then we have to go, and you can have your dinner in peace."

"What?" She came bouncing up out of the chair. Her eyes were flashing as they met Barrabas's cold stare in a frontal assault. "You don't think you're going to leave me behind? Not on your life, pal! This is my territory, and I want to get the job done as much as you, but I want to get it done right. I don't suppose you had anything to do with that trouble down on Bogyoke Street this afternoon."

Barrabas shrugged. "Just doing my job."

"Oh, right...just doing your job! Is there anything to show for it but three men shot? The bodies have already started piling up!"

"We have to leave," stated Barrabas. The four men at the table all stood at once, prepared to follow their leader. Barrabas looked back at Diana. "Bring the files." He turned and walked toward the exit, his men parading behind.

Diana shook her head and watched them for a moment. The waiter returned with a menu and offered it to her. She gave him a stern look, picked up her case and followed the mercs.

The waiter breathed a true sigh of relief. He was very glad to see this party leave. He noticed that they forgot to leave him a tip, but he decided not to complain.

AN OLD HANGAR that had once been used by Burmese Airways was the home of Western Exports and Freight Company. It was located south of the heart of the city, next to the vast piers and docks on the Gulf of Martaban.

Western Exports and Freights had once been owned and operated by Gus Josphet, an ex-Flying Tiger who had remained in Rangoon after World War II to transform his military flight operation into a very profitable business venture. Gus had been one of the many accomplices in the secret shadow wars in Indochina since the turbulent last years of World War II. That part of the world had continued in a state of chaos ever since, and Gus had made a lot of money off the secret players right up until his death a few years previously.

The business was still in operation, being run by Gus's old partner, Sinwa Rap, a sly old Burmese businessman who looked older than the seas.

Garbed in traditional turban and robe, Sinwa Rap stepped out of his cubicle of an office and into the growing twilight. He grinned widely as Barrabas approached. "Ah, Nile. It is good to see you again."

"Hello, Sinwa," said Barrabas, returning the sincere smile. "It's actually good to be back. Do you have my cargo?"

"Indeed. It arrived from Bizerte an hour ago. The Fixer has already called to make sure we delivered on schedule."

"And, as usual, you have not let us down."

Sinwa Rap gave Barrabas a little bow. "Your shipment is inside and ready for your inspection."

Barrabas gave his men a wave, and the four SOBs went into the hangar to receive their cargo. Diana walked up and stood next to Barrabas. He paid no attention to her. "I have some further business to discuss, Sinwa. Can we go inside?"

"Of course." Sinwa Rap politely stepped aside to let Barrabas and Diana enter the office. His dark old eyes were shining with dollar signs. Sinwa Rap's heart and soul belonged in Asia, but his mind belonged on Wall Street.

Diana and Barrabas sat in two chairs in front of a large oak desk cluttered with papers and flight charts. The old Burmese walked behind the desk and pulled out his chair, grinning directly at Diana. "You have such a lovely partner, Nile. I have seen her before."

"Maybe," said Barrabas. "Diana Simone is with the DEA."

"Ah, yes. We have done business with your agency on many occasions."

"I know," said Diana. "I . . . don't ask questions."

Sinwa Rap nodded at her, knowing the people he dealt with belonged to the semi-official departments on the very fringe of her agency. He turned his attention to Barrabas. "So, Nile, word is already spreading like a whore's disease that you are in Burma."

Barrabas chuckled. "I suppose it is."

"The most popular rumor is that you are into drugs. You have come back to set up a business."

"It's something like that," said Barrabas.

"Then you would not be working with an agent of DEA."

"You know it's best not to ask questions, Sinwa. Not when you want to make money."

The old man smiled again and leaned back in his chair, pretending to reflect on what Barrabas had just said. "Yes. And what further services may I perform for you?"

"I need a plane and a pilot. Someone who knows his way around the north country. We may be crossing over a few borders... possibly even into China. I need someone familiar with the locations of the airfields and capable of getting us in and out quickly."

Sinwa Rap beamed. "I have such a man."

"I'll need him tomorrow afternoon," said Barrabas.

"Tomorrow!" exclaimed Diana. "But I have work to do in town. I can't be ready by tomorrow."

"Then stay behind." Barrabas gave her a cold look.

Diana sat back in her chair, her pretty features awash with pure anger.

Barrabas turned back to Sinwa Rap. "The man and the plane can be ready? We will have five passengers... six if Miss Simone decides to go along."

"I'm going!" said Diana, still fuming.

"Six passengers, all with light field gear," stated Barrabas.

Sinwa Rap spread his hands in a gesture of bounty. "Everything will be ready."

"Good," said Barrabas. "You will be paid through the Fixer's usual method."

The door opened behind Barrabas, and Hayes poked his head into the room. "Excuse me, Colonel. I wanted to let you know that the shipment was complete."

"Good," said Barrabas. That was the news he had been waiting to hear. He trusted Sinwa Rap as much as he trusted anyone in that kind of business, but there was nothing to guarantee that somebody wouldn't dip his hands into the stock.

Barrabas stood. "We'll be back tomorrow, Sinwa." He turned and walked out of the room.

Diana stood and quickly followed.

Outside, the sun had almost completely set and darkness was enveloping the night. It was time to go to work.

The SOBs were waiting with their gear: M-16s, a case of M-26 grenades, ammo for the automatics and their various pistols and full web gear. Jessup had not let them down.

Barrabas picked up his M-16, checked it out, rapped a full clip into place and chambered a round.

Standing next to him, Diana watched with wide eyes. "Barrabas! What the hell are you doing?"

"Going to work," said Barrabas.

"What's going down, Colonel?" asked Hayes.

"We're going to pay a little visit to a den of rats," said Barrabas. "We'll go over the plan on our way back to the city."

They piled into the van Diana's agency had provided for them and she got behind the wheel. Barrabas took the front seat next to her. As she started the engine, Barrabas turned around and spoke to his team.

"We're about to launch our own personal war on the Southeast Asian drug trade. This time it's for the kids on the streets."

The four SOBs remained silent. Alex Nanos gave one little nod. Billy Two grinned as wide as he could.

Diana sighed and looked over at Barrabas. "God help the Southeast Asian drug trade."

6

They parked the van on Bogyoke Street, just outside the warehouse district. Barrabas led his team through the maze of alleyways and side streets until they were in front of the rock house where he had conducted his afternoon surveillance.

They crouched in the darkness of an alley and reviewed the plan. "Our target is the dealers," said Barrabas. "We're going in for information. I want to know the direct suppliers and exact locations of where these street distributors are getting their drugs. We go inside, choose a subject, conduct our interrogation and get out."

Diana was standing at the mouth of the alley, looking at the drug den they were about to assault. The building was old and ratty and very dark. Two armed guards stood on the front stoop, guarding the entrance from Bogyoke Street. The open doorway behind them was almost totally black, but Diana could detect or sense movement inside every few minutes. Probably more guards were making rounds through the hallways. Diana had been into many awful places in the course of her career, but nothing quite like this one. Penetration of such drug dens was left up to the special teams who were trained for that type of work and who spent weeks preparing for the job. She wondered what she was doing going into that odious place with a group of crazy mercenaries who had spent less than a few hours conducting surveillance.

"Lord . . . are we really going *into* that place?" She couldn't suppress a shiver.

Barrabas was now standing behind her. "You should wait here. We won't be long."

Diana thought for a moment. She was tempted, but waiting alone in a dark alley off Bogyoke Street at night wasn't really her idea of keeping safe. And she did have her responsibilities. She took a deep breath. "No. I'm going with you. Give me a weapon."

Barrabas smiled tightly. Although he didn't want her along at all, he was almost beginning to like her. She was obviously doing the best she could at a very tough job. He turned and faced his men. "Give her a handgun."

Billy Two gave Diana his Socimi 821 and three spare magazines. "Can you use this?" he asked.

Diana nodded.

"It's light and easy to control. Reloading is quick." Billy gave her a little grin. "Be careful with it—I'm kind of fond of her. Saved my ass a few times."

"You know the plan," said Barrabas. It wasn't a question. "Billy and Diana will come with me. Give us five minutes to get into position in back of the building, then move in. Make it a completely silent assault, if at all possible. The first one who finds any offices or a command center waits for the others. We'll take it together."

The SOBs nodded. They were ready.

"Let's do it," said Barrabas. He gave Diana a hard look. "Stay close to me."

She nodded, took a deep, shuddering breath and fell into step behind Barrabas. Billy was behind her.

They moved back to Anawrahta Road and through a series of narrow side streets until they were behind the drug house. Barrabas moved with ease and confidence, keeping in the darkest areas and not making a sound. Diana remained very close behind. Having him in front of her gave her a measure of reassurance.

The back of the sinister building was not much different from the front. They could barely make out a small yard that was littered with garbage. Armed men walked night patrols around the building, and others were standing inside the doorway. For a minute Diana saw the glow of a cigarette. The night was quiet around them, with the sounds of the city sounding far away, as if that were another world, one of reality that she had left for this nightmare.

Barrabas checked his watch. "Let's go."

Barrabas and Billy Two moved out of the cover of the alley and made their way toward the yard. Diana followed.

The blast of an AK-47 suddenly broke the silence of the night. It was immediately followed by short bursts from M-16s and the shouts of the guards under attack at the front of the building. So much for silent assault, thought Barrabas.

The two guards on patrol outside the building ran in the direction of the firefight. That left the guards inside the doorway. Barrabas and Billy crouched and ran through the darkness, across the yard and up to the building, on either side of the open door. The guards inside had seen a movement, and as they stepped outside to check it out were immediately shot by the waiting mercs. Three bodies toppled into the garbage-strewn yard.

Barrabas looked over at Billy. The Indian grinned. Barrabas nodded. "Inside . . . now!"

Diana had pressed herself flat against the wall behind Barrabas, her eyes nervously darting around. The two soldiers moved on Barrabas's command, going through the doorway together. There were short, sweeping bursts from their M-16s, and then they were inside, lost to the enveloping darkness.

Diana groaned and again followed. She jumped through the door and was suddenly in total blackness. She couldn't see a thing, though she'd always thought she had excellent night vision.

She waited in the dark and choked back a call for Barrabas. A cautious step forward made her consider turning around and running out, but she moved deeper inside. Then a hand grabbed her arm, and she gasped.

"Diana . . ." It was Barrabas. "This way. Stay with me."

She was beginning to see a little. They were moving through a narrow hallway. Barrabas was still holding on to her arm, pulling her along. Billy Two was in front, kicking in doors and quickly scanning the rooms.

As they moved past the busted doors, Diana glanced into some of the dark rooms. She could see kids crouched in corners, shaking and afraid, lying on the floor and high on drugs.

The building was old. The walls had gaping holes and the floor was insecure. In a few spots Diana could actually look down through the broken planks and see the blackness of the basement. Pieces of the ceiling fell on them as they moved past. One naked light bulb burned at the end of the hallway, giving them a destination.

Suddenly the light was broken by a shadow that became a man with a gun. Barrabas crouched in front of Diana, letting go of her arm. "Watch it!"

Billy dashed for cover in one of the rooms as the man at the end of the hall opened up with his AK. From the room behind Billy a girl screamed.

Barrabas opened up on the man with his M-16, and simultaneously Diana fired over Barrabas's shoulder. The man was tossed backward. His AK went out of control, sending a hail of fire toward the ceiling and making the light bulb explode.

"Move!" ordered Barrabas. He grabbed Diana again and pulled her along. Billy came out of the room and charged toward the end of the hallway.

They spotted another man. Diana felt Barrabas tense, and Billy Two stopped running and crouched. The man at the end of the hall turned, and they saw that it was Nanos.

They ran to the end of the hallway to join their comrade. "We had some trouble getting in, Colonel," said Nanos.

"I heard. Where are the others?"

"This way." Nanos led them around a corner to a set of rickety wooden stairs. O'Toole was waiting at the bottom of the steps.

Barrabas walked over to O'Toole. "Where is Hayes?"

"He went up, Colonel. Looking for an office."

Barrabas glanced at the others. "Let's go." He looked back at O'Toole. "Take the rear, Liam."

"Yes, sir."

Barrabas started up the stairs, moving cautiously but quickly. His people followed. Diana stayed next to Billy Two. She was starting to like him. O'Toole was backup, moving slowly behind the others, guarding the rear. One lone red bulb on the wall at the halfway landing lit their way. As they turned up the second flight of stairs, their shadows in the crimson light made strange phantasms dance around them.

They reached the top of the stairs without incident. Hayes was waiting for them at the end of a hallway, flattened against the wall next to a closed door, his automatic ready.

The team moved to Hayes, Barrabas still in the lead. O'Toole stayed at the top of the stairs on watch.

Barrabas approached Hayes and the black merc knew his leader wanted a report. "It's an office of sorts, Colonel. There is evidently a meeting of some kind in progress."

"Dealers?"

Hayes nodded.

"How many in all?"

"Seven. Three dealers and four gunsels. At least five of them are armed with automatics."

Barrabas spoke to the team in very low undertones. "I need one or two of the dealers alive. Don't be choosy at first. Go for the ones with weapons. Let's do this one fast and by the numbers. Ready?"

The team nodded in unison.

Barrabas faced the door. Hayes lay flat on the floor beneath him. Billy moved up on his right. Diana remained against the wall, next to Nanos.

"Go!"

Billy shot the doorknob with his automatic. Barrabas kicked and dove aside for cover. The door burst in, then disintegrated from the rounds of the AK-47s streaming from inside the room and filling the hall with hot lead, tearing the opposite wall apart. All the SOBs stayed under cover against the wall except Hayes. He opened up from the floor with his automatic, sweeping the room with quick, deadly bursts.

In a moment Barrabas and Billy moved. They came from each side of the doorway, their rounds joining Hayes's in cleaning the room. Barrabas and Billy charged inside, their automatic weapon still alive in their hands.

Hayes got to his feet quickly. Nanos joined him, and they also disappeared into the room. Diana was left in the hall, huddling against the wall and listening to the battle. The sound of exchanged gunfire inside the office sounded thunderous to her ears. Men screamed in pain and death.

Then it was quiet. It suddenly became so still that Diana could hear her heart pounding inside her chest. She turned her head and saw Liam O'Toole standing guard at the top of the stairs.

A sound in back of her made her gasp and turn her head around. It was Billy, grinning at her and motioning her into the office.

The place was a scene of bloody carnage. The bodies of the thugs and drug merchants, torn and twisted into odd final positions, were strewn around the room.

A sickening smell filled the air, a mixture of spilled blood and discharging guns that had chewed apart furniture, cloth and flesh.

One drug dealer had remained alive. He was the unlucky one. He sat on a plush sofa, shaking. Alex Nanos stood over him, his M-16 pointing directly at the crook's head.

Barrabas scanned the room, taking a quick inventory. His men were in good shape. Good. Now it was time for business.

Barrabas walked over to the drug dealer, took out his Browning and aimed it at the dealer's groin. He pulled the trigger and blew a gaping hole in the sofa between the crook's thighs.

The trembling man on the couch cried out as the gun discharged between his quivering legs. He saw Barrabas raise the gun two inches.

"The next one will be for real," said the man with the white hair.

"English! I speak English!" said the dealer. "I'll tell you anything! What can I say? What can I say?"

"Start with your name," said Barrabas.

"Xan Nu Pong."

"Chinese?"

"Yes. Chinese. Yes!" The frightened dealer nodded vigorously.

"Who do you work for?" asked Barrabas.

"General Tai Ta Chien."

One of the warlords Barrabas had seen in the DEA's slides. "You handle drugs for General Chien?" asked Barrabas.

"Yes . . . but I just work for him. I a nobody!"

"I'll go along with that," said Barrabas. "Where does the general get his supply?"

"From Ngumla. There is a poppy-growing village in the Kumon Range."

Diana had walked over to Barrabas to watch his interrogation. "I know where that's at. It's far up north, even above the Triangle regions."

"Where can I find General Chien?" Barrabas asked the prisoner.

"There is a house in Rutao—"

Barrabas abruptly yanked the man up, and started to tie his hands with his own trouser belt. He motioned to the others and moved toward the shattered doorway. "We'll continue this later," he was saying, when the sound of automatic fire came suddenly from the hallway.

Barrabas turned to Billy Two. "Check out how O'Toole is doing!"

The SOB warrior immediately headed for the gaping doorway that led out into the hall. He didn't make it.

It was like a magician's trick. One moment the door was open and empty; the next, two black-clad men with AK-47s were filling the exit with death. They opened up on the occupants of the office. It was like shooting fish in a barrel.

"Take cover!" shouted Hayes, diving to the floor.

Only the instincts of men who had spent years at war saved them. The deadly AK rounds sprayed the room, tracers tearing through the darkness with deadly beauty. The SOBs moved, staying alive, grasping for survival.

Xan Nu Pong thought the black assassins were his saviors. He came off the couch, laughing, calling his thanks to them. The rounds hit him with a force that threw his now lifeless body back against the couch and flipped it over.

Nanos and Hayes rolled along the floor, following Barrabas, who was yanking Diana after him and dodging through a rear exit. Only Billy Two was caught in the trap. He had dived to his right to escape the first volley of AK fire, then rolled and come to a quick halt in a corner. He brought his M-16 up to return the fire and took down one of the assassins. The man screamed and fell back into the hallway, and his spot was instantly taken by two others.

The three killers faced Billy, and he knew he wasn't going to get out of this one. He brought his weapon to life on full automatic. He would take as many of the bastards with him as he could!

His return fire distracted the assassins. Their shots were going wild, but only temporarily. The walls around Billy Two were erupting with clashing rounds, paint and plaster and wood exploding over him. He crouched as low as he could, trying to make himself a difficult target. The wall above his head began to erupt, and he realized that someone was tearing a hole in it. A hand reached through and grabbed Billy's arm.

"Billy!"

It was Barrabas, trying to pull him through the wall and into the room behind them. Billy kicked and pushed, trying to use his weight to break through. The three killers stepping into the room to get a clear aim at Billy Two before he was yanked to safety, when the hall was filled with an unmistakable yell. Liam O'Toole flew through the doorway and took down the three assassins.

Billy tried to stand and help his friend, but Barrabas gave a mighty pull and the Osage went smashing through the wall, his body propelled into the other room and almost tossed aside.

Barrabas had Billy to safety, but had to help O'Toole. The Irish SOB was scrapping with the three killers on the office floor. Three against one...usually not bad odds for the fiery redhead. But the three had automatic weapons and were trying to get a bead on O'Toole. They were highly trained killers. And O'Toole was weakening, bleeding from a shoulder wound.

Barrabas couldn't get off a shot with his M-16. It was too much of a risk that he would hit O'Toole. He cursed and leaped through the wall, taking more wooden planks and plaster with him.

Barrabas lurched into the fight, pulling his Browning. He quickly grabbed one assassin by the neck and shot him in the head. He flung the body aside and caught movement in the doorway out of the corner of his eye. O'Toole had one man down and was digging his thick thumbs into his neck. The assassin was gurgling for breath. That one was taken care of.

The other was kneeling, bringing up his AK to shoot O'Toole at point-blank range, when Barrabas delivered a blow to his head with the Browning and shot the assassin in the chest.

The one under O'Toole was gone. The SOB let go and looked toward the door. Barrabas was at his side. It seemed as if the two of them would die together at the command of the tall American who stood at the doorway with two more killers at his side.

"Hello, Barrabas. It's your old buddy, Marshall Edmond. That was a nice fight."

Barrabas calmly looked at the man standing in the doorway. He said nothing.

The killer on Edmond's right lifted his AK to finish off the two mercs, but Edmond pushed the weapon aside with a sweep of his arm. He nodded toward the gaping hole in the wall where Hayes, Billy Two and Nanos were aiming M-16s at them. It looked like a standoff.

"I guess we won't finish now, Barrabas," said Edmond, and he was gone.

Barrabas stood. He wanted to go after them, but O'Toole was in a bad way from loss of blood, and he didn't know the condition of his other men. And then there was the female DEA agent they were burdened with.

Barrabas leaned down to help O'Toole. He lifted his friend with little difficulty and placed a strong arm around his waist for support. "Let's get out of here," he said.

7

General Than Hyut Linh of the Karen Unity Forces in Burma was filled with rage. The early report from one of his runners told him his man had failed in his mission. Barrabas and the Dragon Lady were still alive! They had been in Rangoon all day, allowed to wander around, collecting information about The Seven, and just an hour ago they had successfully raided one of their businesses.

Linh knew that it was not a very serious problem. It was more of an inconvenience than a real threat. Still, he had to confront the nuisance, devote valuable manpower and spend some of his own precious time in dealing with it.

And he wanted the Dragon Lady dead! She had become a thorn in his side, a constant bother to The Seven and their cause. He just couldn't believe they hadn't made enough of a concerted effort to be rid of her by now.

Diana Simone, field agent of the United States' DEA. Informants and her network of various shadow people around Rangoon called her the Dragon Lady. She was Eurasian, and she worked in very unorthodox ways, commanding a virtual multitude of secret agents, listeners and information dealers all over

Southeast Asia. She had come the closest to uncovering The Seven. Her dedicated work had allowed her to put together a surprisingly impressive file on the new cartel's operations in a very short time. She was becoming a continuous bother and obviously had to be dealt with.

She had disappeared from the scene for almost a month, then reportedly had suddenly reappeared with an American mercenary called Barrabas, by her side. That was strange. Why would she be trying to overthrow the cartel to put the American free-lancer into business...unless the United States government was trying to become involved in the Asian drug profits to sponsor their operations here...as it had been rumored they were doing in South America.

General Linh was puzzled, and the more he thought about the possibilities the more he sensed danger. These fools had to be stopped before they could really get down to business. Not just for him, but for the entire cartel.

So General Than Hyut Linh was in a grim mood. Not only had his man failed in his mission to execute the agent and the mercenary, but he now had the pure audacity to stand in that spot, in the most sacred of places, dripping mud! He was a shameless, crude and ignorant man.

"I should have you killed!" said Linh between clenched teeth. His brutal features were twisted with his rage.

Marshall Edmond glared through the darkness of the pagoda's interior at General Linh. "You and the

Queen's grenadiers, Than. Those little boys you have to do your dirty work are a bunch of pussies.''

Edmond had entered the Botataung Pagoda off Strand Road looking for General Linh. He had refused to remove his boots at the door, not caring in the least about Burmese respect for their religious temples. He had wandered through the many chambers, looking for Linh, dripping street muck from his jungle boots, much to the horror of the pagoda's attendants.

He found Linh in one of the ornate interior rooms, whose walls and ceiling were encrusted with semiprecious stones. Edmond felt contempt for his Asian employers, and finding the general in such a place only served to feed that contempt.

By then, General Linh was shaking with uncontrolled rage. ''You dare to enter this place and blaspheme after... after you have failed to perform your appointed duties?''

''Now let's get something straight here, Linh...right from the beginning. I don't take orders from you.''

''You work for The Seven! I am one of The Seven!''

''Yeah. I work for your cartel...it's your cartel that pays me. But I take my orders only from General Chien, your leader. So keep that fact in mind, right along with the idea that I am not accountable to you.''

''Chien wants the problem of the woman taken care of. By now he knows you have failed!''

''And I'll bet he's a lot less worried about it than you are. Hell! You've let your balls get into such an uproar about this thing that you're gonna rupture yourself.''

"You dare to talk to me in such a way...in here...in this holy place..."

"Linh, leave off. Enough of the show. I've come to tell you the real situation."

Linh was shaking even harder. "What...what situation?"

Edmond took a deep breath and let it out in a weary sigh, as if he were trying hard to find some patience with the Burmese general. "Look, Linh, we're dealing with Nile Barrabas. This isn't some pansy-assed toy soldier sent over here by Washington to screw around. This guy is one bad mother, and he could be a serious problem to you and your six associates. Now I don't know what his game is yet, but I'm working on finding out. It appears on the surface as if he's trying to cash in on the opium trade, maybe give your organization some stiff competition. I don't know. All I really know is that he raided your drug house on Bogyoke Street tonight and had a talk with Pong before we could get there and shut him up."

"Did Nu Pong tell Barrabas anything?" asked General Linh.

A look of annoyance crossed Edmond's face. "He told him enough. He told Barrabas about the village and the Ngumla tribes. He was about to tell him about the Rutao estate and probably General Chien, when we got there and shut him up for good."

General Linh clenched his hands into fists, and his eyes glowed with a vibrant rage. "May that little shit's soul rot in the very deepest parts of Hell!"

Edmond chuckled. "Why, General...such language in a holy temple. I sure hope your gods aren't listening right now. You're gonna have to pray the rest of the night just for saying 'shit' in here!''

"Shut up, Mr. Edmond. I am tired of your brash remarks and snide attitude. We pay you good money to act as our enforcer, and you have failed us in the course of a very important mission. You should not be so confident. You are not irreplaceable."

Edmond had no quick comeback for that one. Unfortunately he knew that the observation was very true. And he was beginning to really like his job. He didn't want to lose it. Nor did he want to lose his life, which was probably the quickest, surest way he could be removed from this position.

General Linh spoke again, finally having gained the upper hand in the conversation. "You have failed once. What will you do to ensure that it won't happen a second time?"

"I've learned that Barrabas has chartered a plane and a pilot from Sinwa Rap, which evidently means he's going up to the Kumon Range to check out Pong's story."

"Ah! And you have contacted Wa Duc?" asked General Linh.

"Not yet...but I will. In the morning. And there will be a reception for Barrabas when he goes to the village. The Chief will see to that."

"Good! Good!" General Than Hyut Linh was now smiling. Everything was going to be fine. "And the woman is going with him?"

"I suppose so," said Edmond. "They've been together on this thing so far, even in the raid on the drug house."

General Linh was really beaming his pleasure. "Good! Even better! Chief Wa Duc will kill both of them for us!"

"Not if I can catch them first," assured Edmond. "I'm leaving Rangoon in the morning. I will try to get to Ngumla before Barrabas and the woman to arrange my own modest greeting committee for them." Edmond grinned as he thought about it. "Barrabas and his people won't have a whore's chance in heaven in getting out of there alive!"

8

Somewhere over Naba, or possibly Mawlu, Diana Simone realized she had never been that far north before. They were entering the Kachin State, the uppermost part of Burma. Any farther north and they would be into China and over the Himalayas.

It had been a rough trip up to that point. The twin-prop C-46, one of the last of Gus Josphet's fleet of old World War II relics still in operation, had bumped and thumped and tossed her around on the bench until her behind ached. Next to her, Barrabas and his men took the ride in evident comfort. A few of them slept. Barrabas was reading the DEA reports she had given to him, lost in concentration, totally impervious to the uncomfortable ride.

There were six of them now, including the young pilot Sinwa Rap had provided. They were short one man, O'Toole. He had taken a nasty shoulder wound in the battle at the drug house and was recuperating in a Rangoon hospital. It was certain that he would mend perfectly, and Barrabas had to resort to a direct order to get him to relax and agree to stay behind. He had lost a lot of blood and needed to rest.

They had reported back to the Western Exports and Freight Company in early afternoon. Sinwa Rap had the C-46 and a British pilot named James Emery ready and waiting. Barrabas took only enough time to load up his men and gear and they were off, sweeping north over Rangoon and into the wilds of upper Burma.

They had stopped in Mandalay to refuel and grab some dinner. It was their last chance to eat anything but their field rations for however long it was going to take Barrabas to find the cartel's stronghold and put it out of business.

Late afternoon saw them back in the sky and heading north. By twilight Diana noticed that she wasn't seeing anything out of the porthole but jungle and mountains in splendid isolation. They were leaving Sagaing and entering the Kachin State, some of the wildest country on Earth.

Diana hoped that the pilot knew what he was doing. If they went down in that part of the world, they would almost certainly never be found. If he didn't know where he was going they might end up crashing on one of the treacherous Himalayan peaks. Many a seasoned pilot had gone down to flaming death while flying the famous Hump between India and China. Emery was only in his late twenties and still had a boyish look about him. He didn't fit Diana's idea of a bush pilot, but Barrabas and his men didn't seem to be worried. They obviously trusted Sinwa Rap's judgment.

Barrabas had barely spoken a few brief sentences to Diana during the course of the trip. He was lost in his work, studying the DEA reports, the charts and maps he had obtained from Sinwa Rap and the files Washington had supplied.

To her left sat Billy Two. He seemed to behave the most naturally with her, just friendly and willing to make small talk to help keep her mind off reality. When she let her thoughts take control, she wondered what she was doing, going along with a pack of hard-edged mercenaries hell-bent on a violent confrontation.

She shivered slightly at the prospect, and Billy Two noticed. "Are you cold?"

"No. I was just thinking..."

"Uh! Don't do that, lady. It's not good. Don't think about it...that's the secret. You just go out and do it."

Diana gave him a wan smile. It was the best she could do. She decided to try some more small talk. "I thought there was a woman among your group."

"Yeah, there is," said Billy. "Lee, Dr. Lee Hatton."

"Why isn't she with us?"

Billy shrugged. "She was busy. She's taking some leave. I think she wants to get over losing somebody close to her."

"Oh. That's too bad. It would have been nice to have another woman to talk to."

"You can talk to me." Alex Nanos sat on the bench across from Diana. She turned her head and looked over at him when he suggested they make conversation. By the hungry look and lecherous grin he was giving her, Diana could tell he would like to do more than just talk.

"Yes...quite...thank you, Alex."

"It's too bad we had to leave O'Toole behind," said Billy Two, deciding to change the subject and get

Diana out of trouble. "Those guys were good to catch him like that."

"They were hiding in a room all the time," said Claude Hayes. He was sitting on the bench next to Nanos, looking very depressed. "Damn! I should have spotted them. I just should have known they were there!"

"Hey, it wasn't your fault, partner," Billy told Hayes. "They were trained assassins. It would have almost been impossible to spot them."

Hayes gave Billy a half smile. "Well, I still blew it...."

"Now we know what we're up against." The statement came from Barrabas. He looked up from the chart he had been studying to stare firmly at Hayes. "And Edmond and his men aren't going to let it go at that. They'll be coming after us. We won't make mistakes next time."

"Yes, Colonel." Hayes was looking even more depressed. Next to him, Nanos just shook his head a bit and frowned. Barrabas went back to his work.

Diana turned her head again and stared at the merc leader. He seemed different. Out here, with his men, absorbed in planning the job at hand, he seemed so much more alive and dynamic than when she had first met him in the basement room in Washington. He was now filled with inner strength and exuded purpose. He was strong and full of energy, and Diana sure felt a lot better about him.

Suddenly he looked up at her and spoke, giving her a start. "I just noticed something."

"Well, hello," said Diana. "You noticed that I was sitting here next to you."

"No," said Barrabas. "I noticed that most of the DEA reports are concentrated on the Shan State and the Golden Triangle region. There's very little in here about the Kachin State, or even anything north of the Sagaing border."

"That's right. Our work has been concentrated in the Golden Triangle. The Caravan activity, the supply caches and raw stock houses, the bandit camps and markets, most of the opium tribes and poppy fields...all are located in that region. It's only recently that other clues surfaced."

"Well, that's obviously where you made your mistake."

Anger flashed in Diana's eyes. "Well...pardon us! Years of work down the drain because some adventurer gets a bit lucky, to say nothing about breaking just about every law on the books in the process!"

"I know what I'm doing," said Barrabas.

The C-46 gave another mighty lurch, tossing Diana off the bench. She came back down on her rump with enough force to cause her to give off a loud "Oof!"

Next to her, Billy chuckled. On the other side, Barrabas was still giving her a long, impassive look. She felt sore and wanted to hit something, but she refrained and tried to assume a dignified look.

"I certainly hope you know what you're doing, Colonel Barrabas. Otherwise, this whole thing is well on its way to turning into a crazy nightmare!"

Barrabas didn't answer and continued with his work. The SOBs grinned and suppressed a few chuckles, much to the DEA agent's irritation. Outside, the twilight was quickly turning to night, and the C-46 kept flying north.

EMERY BROUGHT THEM DOWN on a makeshift airfield near the village of Langtao. The field was another relic of World War II, built by the Japanese to transport troops and supplies directly into the heart of their battle with the Chinese and Indochinese.

The air strip was lit by cans filled with burning kerosene so Emery could find his way in through the near dark. The landing was smooth, proving again that the young British pilot was adept at his job. Just the same, Diana held her breath fearfully through the touchdown, certain once again that she was about to die.

When the C-46 came to a stop after a brief taxi, Barrabas stood and ordered his men to unload their gear. Outside, he was immediately greeted by a very friendly, grinning native of the village. He introduced himself as Ba Tat and said he had been expecting Mr. Emery and Mr. Barrabas.

Ba Tat had an old Army deuce-and-a-half waiting to take them into Langtao, where they were going to spend the night. The SOBs loaded up their gear and piled into the truck. Emery got into the cab with Ba Tat to discuss business.

The income of the village of Langtao was supplied almost entirely by crafts made from wood and bamboo. Sinwa Rap had made a deal with the village chief. If they would help Barrabas and his men, the village could send a load of cargo back to Rangoon to be placed in the markets. It was a typical Sinwa Rap deal.

After a rough and bumpy ride in the back of the Army truck, which did absolutely nothing to refresh Diana, they arrived in the center of the small Burmese village. Langtao was typical of one of the northern villages, with its cluster of bamboo huts and wooden shacks. It had become completely dark, and the images of burning torches and shadowy figures of curious natives watching the truck pull to a stop in the village's center only served to fuel Diana's active imagination. She felt as if she had arrived in the Lost World.

Barrabas was again the first to move. As soon as the truck came to a stop, he jumped out and reached for his gear. He began to issue orders. "All right, people. We settle in here for the night. Check your gear and then get some sleep. We leave for Ngumla at daybreak." He turned away and walked into the darkness.

Diana compressed her lips at being left sitting in the truck and not given a rundown of present plans or, at least, a summary of their situation thus far.

It was Billy Two who acted the gentleman, helping Diana from the deuce-and-a-half and offering to carry her gear.

Alex Nanos watched with humorous interest as Billy and Diana walked away together. When they were out of earshot, he turned to Hayes and said, "Billy's sure working hard at getting into that lady's good graces."

Hayes snorted and hauled his gear out of the back of the truck. "Well, he's in for a heartbreak. I think the lady agent has the hots for the colonel."

"Want to make a bet on who tames the Dragon Lady?" asked Nanos.

"Nope," said Hayes, hoisting his pack over his shoulder and walking away.

Nanos grunted and reached for his own gear.

THEY LEFT LANGTAO at daybreak and headed northeast into the Kumon Range region. It was only five miles to the village of Ngumla, but the terrain was difficult to negotiate, and the going was slow.

Ba Tat was acting as their guide. He was one of the few Langtao villagers who spoke some English, and he knew the trails through the bush like the back of his hand.

They moved around the base of towering mountain peaks, through dense jungle and over wet, swampy land covered with decaying vegetation. Overhead, the morning jungle life was beginning to stir, awakened by the intruders. Birds and monkeys cried out, announcing that their domain was being invaded. Insects swarmed around them by the thousands.

Diana wasn't enjoying it in the least. Her American upbringing had spoiled her. She considered herself a devoted city girl. Trekking through this lost world was definitely not her idea of a fun time.

At one point, the small band had to hide behind a fallen rhododendron and lay in silence as a Chinese army patrol marched past. That reminded them how far north they were. They had left all tamed or civilized Burma behind and were now inside a wild, lawless war zone.

It was almost midday before they reached the outskirts of Ngumla. Barrabas called his team to a halt for a quick briefing.

"Nanos, I want you to remain here with the M-16s. We'll keep the side arms, but I don't want to parade in there looking like we've come for trouble. The M-26s we brought also stay with Nanos."

"We're just going to walk in?" asked Billy.

"That's right," said Barrabas. "We haven't come looking for trouble. We only need information. These people grow the poppies to make a living. They don't know they're doing anything wrong. We want to find out who they're dealing with up here, see if they can give us a lead on where the cartel's base is located."

Barrabas turned to Diana. "You can come along to help translate. Keep your weapon." She was still wearing Billy's Socimi in a custom holder on her hip.

Barrabas again addressed the team. "We'll go in single file, Ba Tat in the lead to let them know from the start that we're friendly."

"Okay, boss!" said Ba Tat, grinning and happy that he was turning out to be so important.

Barrabas quickly scanned his team. One by one, he made eye contact with them, then nodded slowly. They were ready. The coming situation was touchy, and Barrabas hoped it wouldn't turn into a confrontation. "All right. Let's do it."

As soon as the little band entered the village area, Diana knew they were in trouble. This was not a Kachin village, like Langtao. It looked as if the villagers were one of the wild tribes of the Kumon Range, tribes who had migrated during the fifteenth century from China to escape the brutal overlords. Possibly Mongolian. They could be Lu or Akha...or Wa. Diana prayed they weren't Wa, the fierce and independent tribe ruled by Chief Wa Duc, a known member of the cartel.

They were being watched by short, muscular men perched high on the strong branches of fame-of-the-forest trees. The watchmen wore only loincloths and peered down at the small procession from behind long, black hair. Their eyes were extremely dark and their faces foreboding-looking.

Diana gave a sideways glance and stifled a gasp. Hanging from a tree were a couple of men...hanging by the neck. She touched Barrabas's arm with a hand that seemed to be reaching for reality.

"I saw," said Barrabas. He kept walking.

Diana turned her shocked eyes on him. "Nile...I think I made a mistake. This isn't just an opium village."

"I know."

"No. You don't understand. I really think I got us into a mess! I think we should turn around. These people are...they aren't nice...."

"It's too late to turn back now," said Barrabas. "They've seen us. We have to go through with our objective."

Diana shriveled inside. Every instinct she possessed told her to turn around and run, but she had no choice. She kept walking next to Barrabas.

They entered the village proper. It consisted of some forty thatched huts loosely arranged in a circle. The path took them into the little court, where they were greeted by staring women and children, all with painted faces.

Ba Tat walked into the very center of the village and stopped. The others halted in a group behind him. A dog jumped over and started yapping at Ba Tat's feet. The Burmese smiled, raised a hand and called out a friendly greeting. He never got to continue. A shot rang out, and a hole was punched through his forehead with a 7.62mm round that took off most of the back of his head as it exited. His lifeless body fell to the ground.

"Oh, hell," said Hayes.

"Sniper?" asked Billy, drawing the 9mm Browning he was carrying in his belt.

"Worse," stated Barrabas, not yet reaching for his Browning.

The beads over the doorway of the hut directly in front of them parted, and a man, obviously a leader, stepped out. Wa warriors, each armed with AK-47s, stood on either side of him.

Diana had never seen Chief Wa Duc in person, only in the recon photos and slides produced by her agents, but she recognized him instantly. Her heart sank to new depths.

"Stupid people!" Chief Wa Duc, grinning, called to them in English. "I have been expecting you!"

The chief waved his arms and suddenly his entire trap was sprung. The enemy appeared from all around, wielding AK-47s, M-1s and even a few F19mm submachine guns. They were mountain bandits, Chinese mercenaries, drug smugglers, Salween River pirates and armed Wa warriors. The scum of the jungle. Barrabas and his team were completely surrounded and grossly outnumbered.

"Uh-oh," Billy Two muttered, looking around.

Chief Wa Duc was joyous that his ambush had turned out so well. He started pacing in a small confined area, as if he were on a leash. Finally he stopped and turned an astonished look on his men.

"Well? What are you waiting for? Kill them!"

Edmond and his team left Rutao around midmorning, moving west at a good clip toward Ngumla. The going was difficult through the thick jungle growth, but their Weisi guide knew the trails.

Edmond didn't like the delay. Upon his arrival at Chien's estate he had been informed that there was a problem to be dealt with immediately. Intruders had been seen on the general's land, and Chien wanted them found and dealt with. Chief Wa Duc could handle Barrabas.

Edmond spent a day hunting down the intruders. He found their camp on the southern edge of Chien's property. Two poachers who had come down through the Pangsau Pass were hunting the land for skins to deal in Bangladesh. Edmond had them killed, then he returned to his original business and the reason he had come up to Kachin: to hunt Barrabas.

As he followed his guide through a thick patch of elephant grass, Edmond couldn't help wondering if he had let Barrabas walk out of the drug den in Rangoon on purpose. Had he let Barrabas live because he enjoyed the idea of having an adversary of talent and respect for once? Was he tired of dealing only with poachers and trespassers on the general's precious land? He smiled when he thought about it. He was enjoying the challenge.

It was an hour's walk to Chief Wa Duc's land and another hour to the village. Edmond didn't allow his men to rest. He pushed them on, hoping to get to Ngumla before Barrabas.

He didn't succeed.

By the time Edmond and his men arrived at the village, Colonel Nile Barrabas was almost a dead man.

CHIEF WA DUC was shouting "Kill them!" when an imperious voice came from the jungle at the edge of the village.

"Wait!"

Edmond and his men strode into the center of the village. He led his men until they came face to face with Barrabas and his people, then stopped.

The renegade American sized up the situation. His mouth quirked in a barely suppressed show of contempt. The chief had called in every available male in the area, anybody with a weapon and a mean face. It looked as though he didn't want to take any chances, but it did seem to be a slight case of overkill.

"Damn, Barrabas," said Edmond. "I sure would have liked to see how you got your ass out of this."

Barrabas looked directly into Edmond's glare with a bland gaze. "It's going just the way I planned," he said.

Edmond laughed, then turned his attention to Diana, placing a hand on her cheek. He felt her jaw clench. "Your little lady here doesn't look so confident. She looks like she could use some help."

"Get your hand off me, you filthy bastard!" Diana's eyes flashed dangerously.

"Oooh! She has spirit. I really like that in a woman. Maybe I'll take her."

"You heard the lady," said Billy Two, reaching out and shoving Edmond's hand away from Diana. "Get away from her!"

Before Barrabas could issue a warning, one of Edmond's men stepped up and hit Billy in the stomach with the butt of his AK, making him buckle up and gasp.

"Back off, Edmond!" said Barrabas, giving his counterpart a hard look.

Edmond waved his man back. By then Chief Wa Duc had appeared by his side, ready to call him to account, judging by the glare in his eyes.

"What you do! Chien radio me and say I to take care of situation! I have everything under control and you come in and screw it up!"

"Don't get into an uproar, Chief," said Edmond. "I just don't want Colonel Nile Barrabas to die so easy."

"I not happy! Not happy at all! I call General Chien and tell him you piss me off!"

"Hey, Chief, you can tell the general anything you want. But he's interested in results, and I always produce. So call him . . . I flat out don't give a shit!"

"You bet I will!" said Chief Wa Duc.

Edmond chuckled. "I think you've been hanging around with those Mandalay whores too much, Chief. You're picking up some nasty slang."

Chief Wa Duc turned around and stormed back to his hut. Edmond turned his attention to Barrabas again.

"So, Barrabas? What shall I do with you?"

Barrabas shrugged. "Why don't we talk about it over a couple of beers?"

Edmond shrugged, and it was clear he was enjoying the situation. "I would, partner, but there're just no open saloons in town."

"Too bad," said Barrabas. "I could use a cold one about now. It's been a hell of a day."

The SOBs stood in silence. Billy could breathe normally again. Diana glanced at Barrabas. She knew what he was doing. He was stalling for time. She wondered if Nanos had gotten lost, or if there was anything he could do. Actually, she admitted to herself, Nanos's chances would be best if he just tried to strike out on his own to save his skin.

"So you work for General Chien," Barrabas stated, still buying time but digging for information now, as well.

"More or less," said Edmond. "He's the top dog of this bunch. There're seven of them in all, warlords and land barons who are working together for the first time in their lives. Chien is the guy who has the most clout, though. It was all his idea in the first place."

"What idea is that?" asked Barrabas.

"The idea to bring all these poppy generals together to increase profits and organize the trade. But there's more to it than that. The general has, shall we say, personal aspirations...."

"Such as?"

Edmond chuckled. "Even though you're going to die, Barrabas, I don't think I should say any more. And by the way...aren't a couple of your men missing?"

"They bought it back in the rock house."

"Uh, I don't know about that...."

Edmond was about to order his men to form a search party, when Alex Nanos struck.

Even in the midafternoon sunshine, the flash of reddish white light given off by the exploding M-26 temporarily blinded Diana. The empty hut on her left suddenly became an inferno as the grenade hit its mark. Nanos tossed a second one as soon as the first went off, and the shack behind the burning hut erupted, spewing hot embers into the sky.

Diana was thrown flat, and Billy landed on top of her. Another explosion made the ground quiver beneath them. She hugged the earth, feeling the tremors, too much in shock even to cry out.

Edmond was bellowing orders when Barrabas hit him. "Grenades! Over there! You men...move out! Move it!"

Barrabas got him with a full tackle that took both men to the ground in a churning, slugging heap. They rolled around, and Edmond was gearing up for a prolonged struggle, but Barrabas had other plans.

The SOB leader elbowed Edmond in the face and quickly heaved off him to jump to his feet. "Hayes! Get to Nanos!"

Hayes was on his hands and knees, scrambling toward the trail out of the village. Nanos suddenly appeared, his M-16 sweeping on full automatic. Three

Kumon mountain bandits went down as they tried to turn and fire back at the Greek devil. Nanos let out a furious yell and threw an M-16 to Hayes. The black merc caught it in the air, spun around and swiftly came up on one knee in a position to fire. He caught two more bandits while Nanos drilled through a pair of charging Wa.

The village was in complete turmoil. Women and children were screaming and running for cover. The heat from the two burning buildings was almost overpowering. Wa men, bandits, drug mercenaries and pirates were blasting in every direction, their leader temporarily stunned on the ground. They were fighting in panic, shooting at anything that moved.

Barrabas was on his feet, his Browning drawn and ready. "Billy! Get her out of here! Get behind Nanos and Hayes!"

"Colonel!"

The Osage grabbed Diana's right arm, and when she didn't respond he began to pull forcefully, lifting her from the ground. "Let's move, lady! This is our chance!"

Diana tried to resist and regain her position lying flat on the ground. She felt safe; she didn't want to be up where she could get killed.

"Diana! Move it! Go with Billy!" Barrabas was crouched, his Browning alive in his grip. He was getting his team out, covering them, once again the last one to leave the fight.

Edmond was disoriented and making attempts to get his bearings. Blood was flowing from his nose where Barrabas had hit him. He shook his head, trying to clear his vision.

Diana forced herself to move. She pushed up and managed to propel herself along somewhat while Billy pulled at her arm as he dashed toward Hayes and Nanos. The two SOBs were covering them with automatic fire, sweeping the enemy and holding them back until Billy and the girl were into the bush.

Barrabas saw the others reach safety and quickly followed. He shot an attacking Wa in the center of his bare chest, the blood streaming over him as the momentum carried the running warrior forward. Barrabas shoved the lifeless body aside and got off another shot, then turned to dash into the brush.

Edmond had regained his feet and was bellowing orders. "Get them! Goddammit! What the living hell are you assholes doing? Move!"

Edmond's team of killers charged into the bush, followed by drug soldiers and bandits. They searched the trail and grounds around the Wa village for the good part of an hour but found no sign of the SOBs.

Barrabas and his team had disappeared.

Edmond was furious, and it didn't help when Chief Wa Duc stormed over, his two mean-looking bodyguards right behind him. "You screwed up! What you do? You crazy!"

"Shut up, Chief. Just shut up!"

"Oh! The general will not like this! No! He will not be happy with you, Edmond! You in a lot of trouble."

The chief was right. Edmond couldn't return to Rutao and tell General Chien that Barrabas had escaped again. Once was for fun, a lark. He had let Barrabas go to enjoy the taste of the hunt. But a second time, right out of the middle of Chief Wa Duc's village . . . Chien would have Edmond executed!

He couldn't go back yet. Edmond and his men couldn't return to the estate until they had Barrabas's head mounted on the end of a stick!

Edmond looked up at the clear sky. He still had most of the afternoon light. Barrabas would be on his way back to Langtao and the airfield. From there, he would regroup, form his battle plan and strike out toward Rutao in search of Chien's estate. Barrabas was clearly on a search-and-destroy mission.

Edmond called to his men. His plan was formed: they would leave right away, not heading back to Rutao, but going after Barrabas!

And this time, Edmond knew, there couldn't be any mistakes! He looked back up at the skies and cursed all the Burmese gods. The only assurance he needed was his own determination to see Nile Barrabas a dead man!

10

They dodged through the jungle in silence, not daring to slow down. They were on the trail for over an hour after their escape from the Ngumla village before Diana could stop shaking. She knew they had barely escaped with their lives. And though the men looked grimmer, their air of calm made her think of Sunday afternoon strolls in the country. But undoubtedly they had a better chance at all times if they stayed calm, she allowed.

She decided to try to follow their example and concentrate on her mission.

She trotted up next to Barrabas, who was leading the group back to Langtao. "Nile...I should thank you for getting me out of there."

"Just doing my job," said Barrabas.

"I suppose I really blew it letting us walk in there like that. I should have known the Ngumla village was Wa Duc's. Most of the land north of Gawai belongs to Duc."

"Most of it," agreed Barrabas. "You've had a lot to think about. If you'd been concentrating, you'd known where we were going."

Diana suddenly stopped in her tracks and glared at the mercenary leader. He'd known all along! She was furious, her fear replaced by anger in a quick wave of emotions. She gave her head a shake and jogged back up next to Barrabas.

"Dammit, Barrabas! You knew! You just let us walk in there and almost get killed! My God!"

"I was doing the job I came here to do. We were covered. Nanos knew what he was doing."

The Greek was walking close behind Diana. He laughed and called to her. "Hey, lady! I wouldn't let anything happen to you. You have to trust us."

"That'll be the day!" Diana shuddered, still thinking about the wrong things. "You sure as hell cut it close, Nanos! We were about to be executed."

"When I saw Edmond and his boys come strolling in, I knew he wouldn't let the chief have all the fun and get all the credit for killing you. I knew I had time."

Barrabas backed his man. "Nanos played it right. He gave me the time I needed to get the information we came for."

Diana thought about that for a moment. She had been so preoccupied with survival that she hadn't realized their mission had been a success.

"We learned that General Chien is the leader of the cartel and their stronghold is located on his estate in Rutao," said Barrabas. "We also learned that Chien has other motives for his drug dealings besides the wealth it provides."

"Probably political," said Diana.

Barrabas nodded. "But it doesn't matter. Our mission is to put the drug cartel out of business by hitting them at the heart of the operation. We'll return to

Langtao and get some rest. In the morning we'll head for Rutao.''

Diana walked in silence next to Barrabas for a while, thinking about how much they had accomplished. Barrabas's methods were certainly unorthodox, but the man did get results.

''I suppose I have to give you guys credit for getting the job done,'' she said after a while. ''But I just don't agree with your methods. I mean...my God! All that carnage!''

Nanos spoke up. ''Hey...I picked my targets very carefully before I struck. No innocent bystanders were hurt. I purposefully didn't endanger any Wa women or children.''

''I wish we could say as much for those other clowns back there,'' said Hayes. He was walking next to Billy in the rear. ''Hell! Those idiots were shooting at everything in sight. I hate dealing with amateurs!''

''Edmond and his men are no amateurs,'' said Barrabas. ''Though Edmond wanted to play a bit of cat and mouse, he won't repeat that performance. And you can bet they won't let this go. They'll be after us...if they aren't behind us right now.''

Diana suddenly turned and looked back with fear. ''You sure know how to make me feel secure, Barrabas. Do you really think Edmond's coming?''

Barrabas nodded. ''That's why we can't waste time. We have to keep one step ahead of them. We'll leave for Rutao the first thing in the morning and try to beat Edmond out of Langtao.''

Diana just sighed and continued the hike in silence. She suffered from acute anxiety for the rest of the trip.

DIANA STEPPED OUT of the hut she had slept in and took a deep breath of the fresh morning air. It was a lovely day. There wasn't a single cloud in the entire blue Burmese sky. She was actually feeling good, until she recalled fully that the mission wasn't over yet.

Although her spirits were somewhat dampened, she felt healthy and strong. She smiled and stretched, then lazily looked around. Mai Su, the villager who had replaced Ba Tat as their guide, saw Diana and walked over to her.

"Good morning, Miss Diana. Colonel Barrabas and the others have already gone to the airfield. He has asked me to take you over there as soon as you are ready."

"Thank you, Mai Su," said Diana. She was still feeling guilty about the death of Ba Tat and wished in a way that she could remain for the evening funeral ceremonies, when the village would grieve his passing. But she had a job to do, and thinking about it quickly put a damper on her good mood.

After a breakfast of fresh fruits and rice, Diana drove with Mai Su to the makeshift airport. Barrabas and his men were giving their field gear a thorough inspection. Emery had just done a final check on the C-46. He saw Diana arrive in the truck and walked over to greet her.

"We're just about set," said Emery, helping Diana out of the deuce-and-a-half.

"Thank you. Where are we going to land?"

"At another World War II airstrip just north of Fort Hertz, about twelve miles south of Rutao. I guess that's where you're going...."

"That's right," said Diana. "Why?"

Emery shook his head, thinking for a moment. "Well, I don't know. That's some pretty bad country up there. All mountains and jungle. Chinese patrols are always coming down across the border. A hell of a lot of people have gone up there and not come back."

"I know this, Jim. But it's my job...."

"Well, if the colonel will let you stay with me—"

Emery never finished his offer to Diana. The explosion behind him made him spin and watch his C-46 erupt into a ball of flame.

"My plane!"

Diana gasped.

Emery turned back and looked at her, and disbelief was mirrored in his eyes. "Jesus, lady...my plane...I—"

It was the last thing he said. Diana recoiled as the single shot took him in the back of the head and his face exploded, spraying her with gore. His body jolted and fell forward, and instinct made Diana grab the corpse and hold it.

"Diana! Get down! Hit the ground!"

She was dazed for a moment, then realized that Billy was shouting at her.

"Get down, Diana!"

The second round buzzed past her head. Sudden shock froze her to the spot as she realized she was holding on to a dead man. She let go of Emery's body and it fell at her feet.

She wanted to scream, but she had no voice. She couldn't move. Another round zipped by her head, even closer this time. She thought she could actually feel the whiz of air.

Barrabas came out of nowhere. One moment she was standing there, overcome by terror, and the next she was in his powerful grip, his tightly muscled arm around her waist, lifting her and carrying her across the open airfield as he sprinted in a semicrouch. Dirt was kicking at his heels as the snipers opened up on automatic, desperately trying to stop Barrabas.

She found her voice and finally screamed. Then she was sailing through the air, gulping to breathe, and Barrabas was in flight next to her, diving for the ditch at the edge of the runway. Diana was tossed, flipped into the air and tumbled very ungracefully into a bed of thick elephant grass.

Barrabas rolled into the trench next to his men. Hayes handed him a rifle and Barrabas immediately came up to return fire at the approaching killers.

Billy was on his right, sweeping over the landing strip with short, deadly bursts from his M-16. "This work sure is hell on pilots, Colonel."

"How many are there?" asked Barrabas.

"Seven, including Edmond," said Hayes, on Barrabas's left.

"He must have brought his whole team," said Barrabas. "What's left of them by now...."

The killer team was trying to advance across the open airfield, but the SOBs had them pinned down. The confrontation had turned into an old-fashioned shooting match, the two sides trenched across from each other, keeping each other pinned down and unable to make a decisive move.

"I have to get behind them," said Barrabas, "or we'll be here all day."

"There's no available cover, Colonel," Billy told him.

"I'll try for a wide sweep. Hell! We can't just stay put in this ditch."

The plane was burning on their left, giving off a massive cloud of black smoke. Barrabas decided to use it for his first move. He ducked and crawled back through the grass, past a rigid looking Diana, keeping as low as his big frame would allow.

One of the killers must have seen him making his move. Rounds began sailing over his head, zipping through the top of the tall grass. Barrabas hugged the ground, again unable to move.

Then something incredible happened. The deuce-and-a-half that had brought Diana to the airstrip suddenly came charging down the makeshift runway, with Mai Su behind the wheel, bellowing like a warrior banshee.

"What the hell's he doing?" asked Nanos.

"Trying to get himself killed," said Hayes.

The SOBs watched the Burmese villager with incredulity, trying to give him some kind of cover fire so he could pull off his unbelievably stupid stunt. They didn't have the slightest idea what he was trying to do.

Mai Su brought the truck to a sudden stop in the very middle of the airfield. He was right between the SOBs and the assassin team, blocking the fire from both sides.

"We still can't move," said Nanos.

Then Mai Su sat up straight in the truck cab, a huge grin on his face and an M-60 in his grip. The killers riddled the deuce-and-a-half with fire, blasting out all the windows and filling the door on the passenger side with gaping holes, but Mai Su just opened up with the M-60, blasting the hell out of the assassins.

"Holy shit!" went Billy Two. "Where did he get that?"

"He must have had it in the back of his truck," said Hayes, still not really believing what was happening.

"Let's move!" said Barrabas. "The little guy's giving us the cover we need!" He was the first one up, jumping out of the thick grass, using the cover Mai Su was providing to charge the assassins.

The three SOBs were right behind Barrabas. They moved to the opposite side of the truck, crouched for action, weapons ready, but there was no need for further caution. Mai Su's deadly and totally unexpected M-60 fire had wiped out the six killers, and their riddled bodies lay lifeless on the ground.

The only one still alive was Edmond, and he was trying to escape.

But Barrabas was onto him.

Edmond reached the edge of the airfield and leaped into the brush for cover. He got caught in a thick thorn bush, cursed and pulled with all his might to tear himself free. He stumbled in his haste, losing just enough time for Barrabas to reach him.

Edmond looked up to see the white-haired mercenary thundering down on him in a snarling, vicious fury.

"Damn you, Barrabas!"

Edmond tried to draw his knife from a sheath, but Barrabas was on him and they were tumbling in the brush. Barrabas forced himself to a halt, digging his jungle boot into the dirt, reaching for the Browning with his left hand while clutching Edmond's shirt with his right. Edmond jerked free and swung at Barrabas, putting the merc off balance for a moment. Edmond pushed himself up to run, but Barrabas was too fast, lurching forward and wrapping his arms around Edmond. They were entangled again, turning over and over on the wet grass, then down a very steep incline, and Barrabas lashed out with his right hand, gripping a vine and holding on in desperation. Edmond screamed a last curse at Barrabas, rolled and went off the edge of the little cliff. He fell headfirst, his arms waving in the air until he hit what looked to be mud.

Barrabas pulled himself to his feet. He looked over the ledge at the swamp where Edmond's boots were sticking up. Edmond was thrashing about, sinking fast.

Barrabas watched the quicksand until Edmond was completely gone. A few bubbles marked the place where he had sunk. Then there was nothing but the flowing muck and a few insects buzzing around the spot, searching for food.

Barrabas looked away, then shrugged and turned to walk back to his men.

ALEX NANOS STOOD by the C-46, chuckling softly as he watched it burn. Diana walked up next to him, still shaking from the ordeal. "What's so funny? I could use a laugh."

"I was just thinking about how mad Jessup is going be," said Nanos. "Now he's gotta pay Sinwa Rap for a plane."

"Yeah. That's hilarious," said Diana. "But did you ever stop to wonder how we're going to get back to Rangoon?"

"We're not going back to Rangoon. At least not yet."

That came from Barrabas. Diana turned and saw him walk out of the brush, looking very tired. She was glad to see he was okay, but didn't let him know her concern. "What are we going to do?"

"We're going to complete our mission," stated Barrabas. "We're going to Rutao to find Chien's estate and put him and his cartel out of business."

"Right. And how are we going to get to Rutao? Our transportation happens to be burning."

"We'll walk."

"Oh, wonderful! We'll walk! About eighty miles of the roughest terrain in the world...to say nothing of the roving drug armies and Red Chinese patrols."

Barrabas shrugged. "It might take us a few extra days, but we'll manage. Edmond and his men did it."

"They knew the territory," said Diana.

"We'll use Langtao guides and scouts," said Barrabas. "Mai Su here will be glad to help us."

The little Burmese hero was standing next to Nanos, grinning proudly, still holding on to his smoking M-60. He smiled at Barrabas and nodded vigorously.

Billy Two and Claude Hayes walked over to join the others. "Where's Edmond?" asked Billy.

"He went for a little swim," said Barrabas. "He won't be a problem anymore."

The SOBs nodded at their chief, knowing the score. Diana shuddered.

"Okay!" Barrabas took command. "Let's get our gear together and load some additional field rations. I want to be on the trail for Rutao before noon."

Diana stood and watched the SOBs go into immediate action. She wished things were that straight forward for her, but there were a thousand doubts and fears in her mind.

She sighed and walked over to the truck, where her gear was still packed. No sooner had they finished doing battle, fighting for their lives, than they were getting ready to march into harm's way once again!

She felt helpless, angry. She wanted to lash out, blame someone for getting her into this mess, but then realized she had nobody to blame but herself. She cursed and reached into the truck for her gear.

11

The cool, wet grass felt good on Sun Ti's bare feet. A tiny tree frog landed briefly on her toes, then jumped high and disappeared in the water. The young girl giggled, enjoying her solitude, though her mood was laced with guilt for coming down to the swamp by herself.

Her parents had told her many times not to go to the swamp alone, especially when night was coming on. It was a place of great danger, a living, breathing thing full of hungry creatures, and the homing place of legends and demons.

The swamp seemed to move about her, a motion comprised of a thousand little movements of insects, frogs, the rippling of water. Ancient fears could not be suppressed. Young Sun Ti could imagine it, the muck and decay rising up and walking like a man. The earth was alive; the marsh was its birthplace. Sun Ti shivered, almost enjoying the moment of supreme fear, tasting forbidden fruit.

Sun Ti had come down to the marsh many times in the past, always alone. She enjoyed having her secrets. She could wander and dream and think of all the things she would have someday... a handsome mate, a home and family, a job in Mandalay where she would make lots of money to support her parents in their old age. Sun Ti wanted a future, a life away from the village. She had never left Langtao in all her twelve years, and when she walked the marshlands south of the village, it was the closest thing to another place and time she could experience.

Yet she always felt the guilt and the fear. The stories the elders told the young children were deep inside her being, always whispering of dangers. Sun Ti enjoyed the solitude and peace and dreams, but she also enjoyed the delicious fear!

Tonight was no exception. She stood in the twilight and looked over the waters, the muck shifting and moving as if it were really alive. She stared into it, thinking about life and birth and the living earth, and she gasped when the hand came out of the muck and grabbed her bare ankle.

The swamp was coming to life! It was reaching out to her! It had eyes peering out of its fetid waters! It had a voice. . . .

"Help me. . ."

The swamp pulled on her, tugging at her life. Her fear was almost subdued, as though all along it had been getting her ready to succumb at the right moment. It almost seemed natural.

"Please . . . help me, girl. . . ."

It was a man. The bog was giving birth to a man-creature. He pulled on her leg for support, drawing himself out of the sucking muck, pulling inch by inch until he was out of it and lying on the solid ground by her feet. He wasn't moving, barely breathing. He needed to be given full life.

Sun Ti cautiously knelt down and touched his shoulder. He gave off a pungent odor. Black mud ran off him, out of him. He needed help. The swamp man needed Sun Ti.

"I will help you."

She stood over him, looking around the growing darkness. The man raised his arm a bit, knowing the girl was going to help him, signaling his thanks.

Sun Ti grabbed several big leaves from some plants and scooped the muck off the man. She made repeated trips to bring in her cupped hands the cleanest water she could find to wash him. She knelt over him, nursed him, cleared his nostrils so he could breathe properly, until his chest was rising and falling in a normal rhythm.

Sun Ti smiled. She was proud. She had brought life from the swamp. They would tell legends of this wondrous thing! She would be popular.

The man sucked at the foul air. He groaned and rolled over. A pool of water that had collected in the small of his back ran into the grass. He used his left hand to wipe muck away from his mouth.

"Who are you?" Marshall Edmond peered up at the young Burmese girl and blinked until his vision was almost clear.

"I am Sun Ti. I am from the village."

Edmond nodded, then started coughing. When he had his breathing under control again, he asked, "Sun Ti...can you find me a drink of water?"

The girl knew where there was a stream. She padded over to it in her bare feet and brought back some cold, almost clean water.

Edmond drank the girl's offering from her hands. It wasn't enough. "Can you take me to where this water is? I must drink and wash."

The girl smiled at him. She reached down to help him up. He was awfully heavy, and still weak. He had crawled through the swamp under the muck for an eternity!

Edmond leaned on Sun Ti and they walked slowly, carefully over to the clear stream. He dropped to his knees and started splashing water on his face and in his hair, drinking some of it, careful not to get more muck down his throat.

Sun Ti stood in the darkness and watched the swamp man. He was white under the mud. He was almost handsome. If only he didn't look so fierce. His eyes were dangerous, cold and shining with hatred. She hoped she had not brought a monster into the world.

After Edmond drank his fill, he slowly turned his head and looked at the girl. His eyes glared through the darkness at her and she shuddered.

"You shouldn't have come here by yourself," said Edmond.

She knew. "This is a bad place," she said, her voice soft and now showing her fear.

Edmond nodded. "But I'm glad you came...and helped me. I might have died."

"Weren't you born of the swamp?" asked Sun Ti.

Edmond laughed. "Born, no. Resurrected, maybe...."

Sun Ti sighed. Well, a resurrection was better than nothing.

"Can you get me some food?" asked Edmond.

"If you will come back to the village with me."

"No. I can't go to the village. Can you bring food to me here?"

Sun Ti shrugged. "I will try."

She would have to sneak the food out of the village. Her parents would never let her get some food and return alone, in the night, to the swamp, especially if they knew a swamp man had been resurrected. They would hold her back and village men would go looking for the man.

Sun Ti didn't want that. The swamp man belonged to her!

It took her the best part of an hour, but Sun Ti was eventually able to snatch some food from the village and deliver it to Edmond. She brought fresh fruits, cold rice and raw fish. It wasn't really the meal he would have preferred, but he devoured everything.

Sun Ti sat and watched her swamp man eat the food. The night had enveloped them, and the night rustled with sounds of the nocturnal swamp life. The Burmese jungle was not the place to be after dark and Sun Ti knew she should return to her home. Her parents would already be furious with her for staying out this late. They were probably looking for her around the village by now. And even with a swamp man to take care of her, Sun Ti was starting to become edgy. She knew what terrible things the night could spawn.

"I must return home now," said Sun Ti.

"What?" asked Edmond, finishing off the last grains of the rice.

"I have to go back to the village. My parents will be worried."

Edmond swallowed. He scooped up some more of the cold spring water and drank deeply, washing down the meal. "I'm sorry. I can't let you do that."

"But I must!" insisted the young Burmese girl. "I would like to remain here with you, swamp man. I like taking care of you. But I must return."

"No. You don't understand. You can't tell anybody I'm out here. That you found me and that I live."

"Oh, I will not tell!" Sun Ti assured him. "You belong to me. You will be my secret."

Edmond chuckled. With burning eyes he glared through the darkness at Sun Ti. They were the eyes of a man who had lost all reason, the eyes of a man overpowered by an insane purpose. He had been defeated. His team had been destroyed. His mission had been thwarted. And he had been shoved into the slime to die.

But from that primeval mire a new being had been born...a being with one purpose in its life: to destroy the man who had done this to him! Nothing would or could stop him. He would accomplish his one goal, even if it meant hurting innocents.

Edmond turned to Sun Ti, reaching for her. The young Burmese girl didn't even have a chance to cry out.

SUN TI'S BROTHER, Than, found her body early the next morning. His cries of despair alerted the others in the search party. They came running to his side and wept when they saw the fate that had befallen her.

A wild beast had mutilated the poor young girl. A night creature of the bog had caught her and lustfully killed her. They would think that something inhuman had hideously cut short Sun Ti's life.

They were correct.

12

The Kumon Range area of northern Burma is mountainous, jungle covered and extremely isolated. It is the scene of a continuous drug war, filled with dangers and the means for sure, sudden death. Diana Simone thought it absolutely the last place on the face of the Earth she would pick for a cross-country hike.

Barrabas and his team were on the trail to Rutao for the better part of three days. They had to stay under cover in the bush and keep off the trails for fear of being detected by one of the roving drug armies, Chinese border patrols or any of the many bandit groups hiding out in the mountains. Their progress was slow, the march often tedious and rough, but Mai Su and the Langtao scout assisting them knew the way.

It was nearly sundown of the third day on the trail before they reached Rutao. Barrabas led his weary team into the town, which consisted of a trading post and a tavern.

"I wonder if it's Saturday night," said Nanos. "We might find some action."

"I think it's only Thursday," stated Hayes.

"Ugh!" Nanos grunted. "I wonder what Rutao women do on a Thursday night."

Deal Yourself In and Play

GOLD EAGLE'S

ACTION POKER

Peel
off
this card
and complete
the hand
on the
next
page

It could get you:

♠ 4 Free books

♠ PLUS a free pocket knife

O BLUFF! NO RISK! NO OBLIGATION TO BUY!

Play "Action Poker" to see if you can get

♦ 4 hard-hitting, action-packed Gold Eagle novels just like the one you're reading — FREE

♦ PLUS a useful pocket knife — FREE

Peel off the card on the front of this brochure and stick it in the hand opposite. Find out how many gifts you can receive ABSOLUTELY FREE. They're yours to keep even if you never buy another Gold Eagle novel.

Then deal yourself in for more gut-chilling action at deep subscriber savings

Once you have read your free books, we're willing to bet you'll want more of those page-crackling, razor-edge stories. So we'll send you six brand new Gold Eagle books every other month to preview. (Two Mack Bolans and one each of Able Team, Phoenix Force, Vietnam: Ground Zero and SOBs.)

♦ Hot-off-the-press novels with the kind of no-holds — barred action you crave.

♦ Delivered right to your home.

♦ Months before they're available in stores.

♦ At hefty savings off the retail price.

♦ Always with the right to cancel and owe nothing.

You will pay only $2.49 for each book — 11% less than the retail price — plus 95¢ postage and handling per shipment.

Enjoy special subscriber privileges

♦ With every shipment you will receive AUTOMAG, our exciting newsletter FREE.

♦ Plus special books to preview free and buy at rock bottom discount.

Yours FREE — this stainless-steel pocketknife.
Talk about versatile! You get seven functions
in this one handy device – screwdriver,
bottle opener, nail cleaner, nail file, knife,
scissors, and key chain. Perfect for pocket,
tool kit, tackle box. Turn up four aces on the
card below and it's yours FREE.

GOLD EAGLE'S
ACTION POKER

Peel off card
from front and
place here

Check below
to see how many
gifts you get

Yes! I have placed my card in the hand above. Please send
me all the gifts for which I qualify, under the conditions
outlined in the attached brochure. I understand I am under
no obligation to purchase any books.   166 CIM PAN6

Name

Address

City _____ State

Zip Code

Four Aces get you 4 free books   Full House gets you   Three-of-a-kind
and a free pocketknife   4 free books   gets you 3 free books

PRINTED IN U.S.A.

Terms and prices subject to change. Offer limited to one per household and not valid for present subscribers.

Gold Eagle No Bluff, No Risk Guarantee

● You're not required to buy a single book—ever!
● Even as a subscriber, you must be completely satisfied or you may return a shipment of books and cancel at any time.
● The free books and gift you receive from this ACTION POKER offer remain yours to keep — in any case.

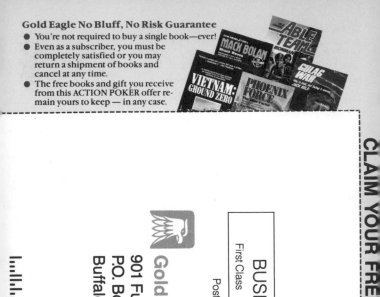

CLAIM YOUR FREE GIFTS! MAIL THIS CARD TODAY.

BUSINESS REPLY CARD

First Class   Permit No. 717   Buffalo, NY

Postage will be paid by addressee

Gold Eagle Reader Service
901 Fuhrmann Blvd.
P.O. Box 1394
Buffalo, NY 14240-9963

NO POSTAGE
NECESSARY
IF MAILED
IN THE
UNITED STATES

They went into the tavern, a place called Viper's Hole.

"I wonder how it got a name like that," said Billy Two.

"I don't know," said Hayes. "But I suggest we watch where we step."

The inside of the tavern was dark and filled with smoke. The air was foul and pungent. There was more being smoked here than tobacco. Diana squinted against the darkness and her eyes started to water. She couldn't see a thing. She placed one hand on Billy's back to find her way to the table Barrabas had selected.

The SOBs shuffled their chairs and sat down so their backs were to the walls. Mai Su and the other Langtao native sat down grinning. This was a real outing for them.

The wooden table looked as though it would fall apart at any moment. The mercs carefully placed their weapons on the table and their gear on the floor. The group was covered with dust and sweat from their long days and nights on the trail. They looked like hell.

Diana felt even worse than the others looked. She sighed hard, feeling a sudden and almost overpowering wave of depression. It occurred to her that she could have been back in Rangoon, and that very night going to a show or having dinner at the hotel. But there she was, instead, in hell's backyard with a bunch of hard-bitten mercenaries, searching for the estate of a Chinese warlord! She seriously questioned her sanity. But, then, she was the know-it-all who had insisted on coming along.

The bartender, a gruff, filthy-looking individual, also served as the tavern's only waiter. He walked over to the table and grunted at them. Barrabas ordered beers.

"So what are we doing in here?" Diana asked after the bartender had left with their orders. "I mean...what are we going to do, just ask where Chien's estate is located?"

"That's right," said Barrabas.

Diana looked at him as though he were crazy. It wasn't the first time she had given the merc leader that look.

Before she could ask if he had lost his mind, the bartender returned and placed seven bottles of beer on the table. He asked if anyone wanted a glass, and they all declined. Diana shuddered at the thought.

The six men grabbed the bottles and began guzzling. The beer was warm but wet. Diana cautiously tasted hers, and screwed up her pretty face with disgust. She had to force herself to swallow the amber liquid. It tasted like warm...urine.

She put her bottle back down on the table and pushed it away. Mai Sui, who was sitting on her left, had already finished his brew and announced his satisfaction with a tremendous belch. He saw that Diana didn't want hers and asked if he could have it, then hungrily guzzled the second bottle.

Diana turned her attention back to Barrabas. "So what were you saying? We're just going to ask for directions to Chien's estate?"

"That's right," said Barrabas.

"Now why didn't I think of that? What a novel idea. Let's just tell everybody in Rutao that we've come to smash their little drug business. That'll make us real popular...."

Barrabas took another swallow of his beer and stood. He walked over to the bar and called to the bartender. Diana watched as they conversed briefly and Barrabas reached into the pocket of his bush jacket and pulled out a wad of kyats. He paid the bartender for the drinks and peeled off more bills to encourage the sharing of information. The bartender stuffed the money into the pocket of his dirty apron, then talked to Barrabas for a long while, pointing north and waving his arm around a bit. Barrabas listened until the man was through, nodded at him and returned to the table.

"Let's go."

The SOBs and Langtao warriors stood and reached for their weapons and gear. The only one who asked a question was Diana. "And where are we going?"

"To Chien's estate," said Barrabas. He turned and stalked out of the bar.

BARRABAS FACED Alex Nanos. "You know what to do." It hadn't been a question.

"No problem, Colonel. You can count on me."

Barrabas looked lost in thought for a minute, then continued. "When you get as far as Ledo, on the other side of the Pangsau Pass, you'll be able to obtain transportation to Nepal. Remember to ask for Colonel Calvert of the First Battalion. He's expecting you."

"Right, Colonel."

"We'll be ready for you in five days. That should be enough time." Barrabas didn't mention that if Nanos didn't return in the allotted time, it meant he didn't make it.

Nanos gave Barrabas his most reassuring grin. "I won't let you down, Colonel." Nanos knew that failing in his assignment would mean certain death for his teammates.

Barrabas placed a hand on his friend's shoulder in a brief and rare display of compassion. "Godspeed, Alex...and good luck."

Nanos nodded to his leader. He wouldn't fail this man. He turned and signaled the two Langtao warriors, and they disappeared back into the bush.

Barrabas turned and went back to join the others. "You'll bivouac here for the night."

"Here?" Diana said incredulously.

Hayes and Billy Two didn't ask questions. They began setting down their gear.

Barrabas fixed Diana with a steady gaze. "Yes. Here."

She turned around and looked down on one of the most incredible, terrifying sights she had ever seen. They were on a grassy hill in a small clearing surrounded by brush. Beneath them, about an eighth of a mile away, was the estate of General Tai Ta Chien.

Diana turned back and looked at Barrabas. "You said 'you'll' stay here. What does that mean?"

"It means you'll get some rest," said Barrabas. "Claude and Billy will take turns on watch during the night. You can sleep."

"And what will you be doing?"

"I'm going in for a look around."

"'Going in'?" Diana echoed. She thought that was absurd.

"Yes," said Barrabas, trying to be patient. "I'm going to use the darkness to conduct a surveillance."

"But you can't go down there alone! My God…did you look at that place?"

"Yes," said Barrabas, still exuding patience. "And I intend on taking a much better look. You would understand if, contrary to my expectations, you weren't such a rank amateur. And you are a DEA agent!"

Diana knew he was right on more than one count, though her job had been to assemble facts behind a desk. There was no use trying to talk him into changing his mind, because he had no choice, she realized. Events were starting to roll along.

But she knew that going into Chien's estate would be suicidal.

The grounds of the estate covered four or five acres of land, all grass, shrubs and gardens. The lawns were immaculately manicured, groundskeepers working even now in the growing twilight. The very jungle had been excavated to create a beautiful home for what must be a very vain man. It was more than obvious that General Chien liked his comforts and insisted on extremely lavish surroundings, even in the heart of Burma's wild Kumon Range.

In the center of the rolling grounds was Chien's house, a massive home that seemed like a brooding menace, though certainly no expense had been spared to make it resemble a monarch's or ruler's fitting residence. The mansion was lit, and it glowed against the rising darkness. Judging by forms and shadows moving in the windows, there was a lot of activity going on inside.

The terrifying aspect of Chien's estate was that although it looked like a farm, instead of barns and stables, the grounds were adorned with militarylike barracks. And instead of livestock of some kind, the estate harbored men. Dangerous men. Mercenaries, bandits, drug dealers, pirates. The lowlife of Indochina. They roamed freely, some drinking and carousing, some with women. The ones on guard duty stood their posts or walked the perimeter. All of them were armed.

Chien's estate was a virtual fortress.

Diana felt duty bound to try to talk Barrabas out of the reconnaissance, but Barrabas turned and walked away from her in silence.

Diana felt extreme helplessness. She took a step after the mercenary leader but stopped when she felt a hand on her shoulder. The grip was gentle but firm.

"Let him go, Diana," said Billy Two.

"But he'll get killed!"

Billy chuckled. "The colonel knows what he's doing. He does these things. It's what makes him tick. Why don't you come over here with Claude and me and get comfortable. It'll be dark soon and we should settle down."

Diana looked forlorn. She was still frustrated. "I know it's his job and I realize I must sound like a silly woman to you. But I do worry about him. Shouldn't one of you go with him to back him up or something?''

''No, Diana. Just come over here with me.'' Billy pulled gently on her arm, leading her to where Hayes was sitting. It was a small clearing where they could stretch out and get some sleep through the night.

Diana let Billy take her to a log and set her down. ''Relax, kid,'' he told her, grinning with reassurance. ''It's going to be a long night.''

''We're just going to sit here?''

''That's right,'' said Hayes. ''That's what the colonel told us to do.''

Billy sat on the log next to her. ''Don't worry, Diana. It's just something the colonel does, a response to an inner challenge. It's almost spiritual. He becomes one with the night, a part of the darkness. He'll go down there and do his job, and he'll be back in the morning. We've learned to accept it, and wait.''

''That man just makes me nervous.''

Billy chuckled again. ''He has that effect on everyone. But, like I told you in the plane, don't think about it. The colonel is good at what he does, maybe the best. He learned it in Nam, going out alone on mission after mission into enemy territory. He had a knack for it, like it's his purpose.''

''Yeah,'' said Hayes. ''And when they stuck the colonel behind a desk in Saigon, it was like tearing his soul out and locking it in a box. He longed to be back out there, in the kind of place he's in tonight.''

''It's a strange way to get your kicks,'' said Diana, giving her head a little shake.

Both men laughed softly. "I suppose," said Billy. He was glad the young woman was finally relaxing a bit. She would need the rest.

"You men seem very loyal to Barrabas," said Diana, looking into Billy's eyes. "Isn't that kind of odd for mercenaries? I mean, from what I understand about the breed, mercenaries only have themselves at interest."

The two men did not seem to be offended by the girl's remarks. "I think we stopped being mercenaries a long time ago," said Billy. "Sure, we get paid for what we do. So does every soldier. But there's something now that goes beyond the money. I mean, each one of us could retire at any time. We have all made enough money to live the rest of our lives very comfortably. It's just all become something more."

"Yeah," said Hayes. "It's hard to explain. When the colonel recruited me to join a dirty tricks team under contract with a free-lance outfit, hell, I jumped at the chance. It was just what the doctor ordered for me at the time."

"I felt the same," said Billy. "All the money and regular work...and just stay alive for a few years and I could retire a wealthy man. It was all too good to be true. But since I started this work, serving under Colonel Barrabas, I look at it all very differently. I feel that my life means something, that I'm really here to do some good."

Hayes grinned. "I have those same strong feelings. And the reason is the colonel. I mean, like what he said to us in the van when we were going to the rock house in Rangoon. He said, 'This time it's for the kids.' Hell, that was all it took. He touched our buttons. Suddenly we weren't doing it for the money or even for the DEA. We were doing it to save the lives of the kids. Our work had meaning, and we had the motivation to go into that place and get the job done.''

"Exactly!" Billy showed a flash of white teeth. "The man is a born leader.''

That seemed to sum things up, and they sat in silence, each lost in private thoughts. The darkness had set in and the bush around them was coming to life with the sounds of the night.

Diana was starting to feel at peace with the world, more relaxed than she had been in days. She felt that she wasn't spending the night with a couple of money-hungry mercs. They were men who had the same sense of morality about their work that she did about hers. For the first time, she experienced a sense of kinship with these guys. And it made her feel good, because what they were doing was right. Every soldier wants to feel this when he puts his life on the line...that his task is all-important and really means something. That the fighting and dying have a purpose and the world will be better because of them.

"Anybody want some chow?" asked Hayes, reaching into his pack for a can of beans.

"Sure," said Billy. "Then I'll take the first watch and you guys can get some sleep. Tomorrow could be a busy day.''

After a meal of beans, dried beef and crackers, washed down with water from their canteens, Diana and Hayes found a soft patch of grass and settled down for the long night. Diana couldn't stop think-

ing about how the two soldiers had described their relationship with Barrabas. She felt so much better
about what she was doing now. From the beginning of
this assignment, she had very mixed feelings about
working with a pack of mercenaries. She had realized
that the situation was grave and people were going to
have to die, but it had still felt very dirty to her.

Now it was different. It felt clean, as if what she was
doing was right. These men were actually trying to
make a difference and do some good, put some
meaning in their lives and make their time on Earth
count. Those emotions and feelings mirrored her own.

She was surprised when sleep easily approached her.
She must have been more tired than she had realized.
She sensed the soft waves of sleep taking her down and
she let herself go with a last thought of reassurance.
She was doing good.

HER DREAMS were of rolling meadows and wind-
swept grasslands. It was a beautiful country setting,
and she was walking free and easy over the hills of
soft, sweet-smelling grass. Beautiful horses were
grazing about her. She was at peace amid a scene of
calm beauty.

But something was very wrong in her Eden. The
horses were acting up. They looked at her and their
eyes were red with fire. They were all black, demon
steeds, turning toward her. They reared up on their
hind legs and began to metamorphose, becoming human...turning into men with weapons aimed at
her...pulling the triggers—

She came awake with a tremendous start. She opened her eyes, and one of the demons was looking down at her!

Diana opened her mouth to scream, and the demon's hand shot out and covered her mouth, muffling the cry.

"Diana! Easy...take it easy," said Barrabas.

"Oh, Barrabas! Don't ever do that to me again!"

Barrabas looked hideous. His face was streaked with black camouflage grease. His hair was darkened and slicked down to his skull. He was filthy from crawling through the brush and dirt, and he smelled of sweat and jungle muck.

"Sorry I scared you," he said. He sat back on his haunches and Diana sat up to face him. "We're getting ready to make our next move."

Billy and Hayes were already up and getting their gear together. Diana looked around at the men and rubbed the sleep from her eyes.

"How did it go last night, Nile?" she asked, her mouth dry and her voice still thick. "Did you find out everything you wanted to?" She reached for her canteen.

"I learned enough," said Barrabas. "I know the layout of the estate and where the best cover on the grounds is located. I found the weak areas of their perimeter defense, how the guard shifts are structured through the night and where the largest fortification of the enemy is located. I am familiar with the layout of the team houses, both inside and out. I was in one of them.

"I know how the house is guarded and how many men are on duty inside and out. I also learned that there will be a very important gathering of the cartel bosses in a few days."

"You learned all that in one night?"

Barrabas smiled slightly and was about to speak, when Diana put up her hand. "I know... I know... you're good at what you do. I 'm tired of hearing it." She stood and stretched. Despite the fact that she had slept on the bare ground and had had jarring nightmares, she felt rested. She took a deep breath of the cool, morning air. "What is our next move?"

"We're going down to Chien's estate and apply for work."

"Excuse me?" She was positive she hadn't heard him correctly.

Barrabas shrugged. "You know what they say. If you can't beat 'em, join 'em."

13

Alex Nanos and the two Langtao warriors made nearly five miles on the first evening before it became too dark to travel safely through the jungle. They found a small clearing by a stream and rested until daybreak. At the first light they were up and again heading southwest on the first leg of their trek to Pangsau Pass.

They had no problems apart from a few pesky insects on the first morning. Mai Su was acting as the primary guide. He had been born and raised in this land and knew the terrain fairly well. The other native, Bo San, was acting as scout. He would move quickly ahead of the others and return periodically to report on any possible dangers or obstacles along their path.

Their luck held out until midday. They stopped to rest and have some rations, taking the usual half hour break. During this time, a Chinese patrol moved down from the north and headed east along almost the same route Nanos and his men were on.

After the rest and lunch of rice balls and pork, Bo San jumped up and scurried on ahead of the others. Nanos and Mai Su roused themselves and began gathering their gear. They were just about ready to leave the resting place, when Bo San hurriedly returned.

He was very excited about something. "Trouble! Trouble! Patrol of Chinese soldiers coming directly in front of us. They be right here in short time!"

"Did they see you?" asked Nanos.

"No," said Bo San. "I do a good job. They did not see me."

Nanos quickly checked the area to be sure they weren't leaving any signs behind. Satisfied there were no telltale traces, he motioned the others to follow him and pushed into a thick patch of brush.

They found a gully completely covered by thorn brambles and vines and slipped under the natural covering into the grassy ditch.

After years in the field and on various war fronts, Alex Nanos's senses had been acutely sharpened, and he could almost feel the Chinese patrol as it approached. Then they were there, almost directly overhead, passing in single-file formation. About nine of them, armed.

The three men in the gully held their breaths and kept completely motionless until the patrol was well past and heading east along the seldom used trail. When they were gone, Nanos let his breath out and grinned. He motioned to the others, and they climbed out of the hiding place.

What they hadn't known was that there was another patrol close behind the first. Bo San had only spotted the one group before returning to warn his comrades. Chinese squads travel in pairs, and shortly after the first had passed them, the second patrol came along.

Unfortunately it came just as the three men were climbing out of the gully.

Nanos saw them first. "Shit! Take cover!" He gave Mai Su a shove and dove behind him back through the thorns and into the ditch. His bush clothing caught and tore and his arms and face suffered a dozen small but nasty lacerations.

Bo San followed in a headfirst dive through the thick vines. He hit the grass on his back, rolled and came to a sudden stop against the opposite side of the gully.

Someone shouted above, then the brush and grass erupted around them as the soldiers opened up with the AKs on full automatic.

"Damn!" said Nanos between gritting teeth as chunks of dirt and sod sprayed onto his face. They'd have to fight their way out of the encounter. The Chinese patrol was obviously of the "shoot first, ask questions later" variety.

Nanos knew that the AK type 56 automatics were very dangerous weapons. The 7.62mm rounds were thumping into the dirt and foliage around them. Some of them evidently had the Type 56SA carbines, and would have the disadvantage of the bulkier, less effective weapon. If he had to fight, Nanos would try to take out those with AKs first.

The SOB warrior had his M-16 and the two Lang-tao natives had their M-1 carbines. Not much of a match for a well-armed Chinese border patrol. What might tip the scales was that Nanos had the M-26 grenades.

"Wish I still have my big 60 gun," said Mai Su. "Then I give these guys some real shit!"

"It would have been too bulky, Mai," said Nanos, only half thinking about what he was saying to the native. He was concentrating on his next move. "We needed to be able to move quickly through the terrain. The whole idea was not to get caught."

"Ha!" said Bo San. "We sure screw that up!"

Nanos thought for a moment more, allowing the Chinese fire to let up a bit. When it was quiet above, he gave a command. "Okay! Let's return some fire and show these bastards we have some teeth. We want to keep them at a distance."

Nanos lurched up with the two warriors at his side and peered over the edge of the ditch. The Chinese were only half under cover. They must have thought they had some helpless bandits trapped. Well, Nanos would show them what they had!

"Now!"

The three soldiers brought their weapons up and opened fire. Diving for cover, the enemy scattered. Nanos saw at least two of them take hits and go down screaming.

Suddenly the ground and brush around them began to explode with new fire, but it was coming from behind them, from the other side of the gully. Nanos and his two men dropped back into their cover.

"Jesus! The other patrol must have come back!"

Sure enough, the first border patrol had heard the firefight behind them and had returned to investigate. They had arrived on the scene just as Nanos and his men had popped up and begun returning fire at the rear patrol. The Chinese squad leader immediately gave the order to join the battle and now Nanos and his men were caught in a vicious crossfire.

The earth and brush around the three men blew apart as rounds buzzed over their heads. They had to flatten themselves against the wet ground at the bottom of the gully and were barely able to move.

Nanos waited. The fire continued for a long time, then began to peter out to almost nothing. Nanos was thinking desperately that they had to make a move soon.

"We have to return fire," he told the others. He was about to give the command, when he heard a shout from above. It was in Mandarin Chinese. These guys were hard-core! The situation couldn't get worse, Nanos thought.

But it did. The Chinese opened up again from both sides of the gully, but this time the fire was coming from a closer range and on both sides. The two patrols were moving up on them. Nanos and his men were caught in the middle.

"Shit!" said Nanos, digging himself into the mud again. "Trapped like rats!"

Bo San guffawed. "Ha-ha! That a funny one! Trapped like rats! You just make that up?"

Nanos looked at the grinning man as if he were insane. He just shook his head and hunkered down in the muck.

But Mai Su was near panic. His features showed the strain. "We going to be dead rats in a minute! We really buy it this time!"

Nanos cursed again. His head was reeling. The Chinese were moving closer on both sides. Sod, dust and torn vegetation rained down on them, the results of the deadly crossfire.

It was time for an act of pure desperation. Nanos yanked two of the M-26 grenades from his web harness and pulled the pins. He rolled onto his back and waited.

The dirt peppered down on his face. Nanos gritted his teeth and spoke in a low and deadly voice. "Come and get it, you sons of bitches!"

The two Langtao natives looked at the crazy man, their eyes wide with terror. They knew they were about to die!

14

Barrabas led the remains of his team through the main gate of Chien's estate and marched onto the grounds. Bandits and drug soldiers instantly started to take a lot of interest in the intruders. They walked over and stared at Barrabas and his companions, grinning, whispering and shaking their heads.

Diana was of particular interest to the assortment of criminals. She felt as if she were being sized up for dinner, although she noted that there were a lot of other women around. But she was a new item to ogle. She stayed very close to Barrabas, and Billy Two walked close behind her.

The days of stress in their search for Chien's estate had taken their toll on the small band of warriors and the weariness and fatigue showed. They looked tired and filthy, like a patrol just in from a long recon mission into enemy territory. Which, in fact, was exactly what they were. The only difference was that this team wasn't returning to the safety of a camp or firebase. Barrabas was marching his people brazenly into the enemy's stronghold.

Barrabas had explained the plan to Diana. They would penetrate the enemy by joining forces with him, and thus be in position to strike from the inside. The plan made a lot of sense. It also held a huge amount of room for error, and they could very easily end up dead.

But she had come this far, and she had to stick with it, which meant trusting Barrabas's judgment as the leader and heading with him into the fray.

Barrabas led his tiny band into the center of the property, following the main walk to the house, then came to a halt. The bandits and jungle lowlife surrounded them, brandishing assorted weaponry. Barrabas waited for one of them to speak.

They stood and waited for about two long, shuddering minutes. Finally a fat, gruff individual who looked as though he belonged in a pirate movie stepped out of the pack.

A bandana around his forehead held back his long black hair. He stepped very close to Barrabas and purposely stared at him with a very intense and penetrating gaze. Barrabas didn't flinch. The man was evidently one of the more powerful bandit leaders and looked Mongol.

The Mongol stood and continued with his inventory of Barrabas, then demanded with a grin, "Are you crazy?"

"We've come to work for General Chien," stated Barrabas.

"Ha! You wish to supply entertainment? You wish to give us a few good hours while we skin you and cut you into pieces and have the woman many times?"

"It wasn't what I had in mind," said Barrabas. "I am Colonel Nile Barrabas, and have killed Captain

Edmond. The general will be needing another enforcement team. We have come to apply for the job.''

"You killed Edmond?"

"That's right."

"Ha! You must be one tough son of a bitch!"

"I am," stated Barrabas.

"You think you are tougher than these men you see here, who want to kill you now?"

Barrabas gave the bandit leader one of his sort-of smiles. "I could take this bunch of clowns out in my sleep."

"Ha!" The bandit punched Barrabas in the arm in a friendly gesture. "You are one nervy bastard, Colonel Barrabas. I think I will kill you myself."

"Before you make any definite plans, don't you think you'd better consult with the general? He may have other ideas. I'm serious when I say he can use our services. With Edmond gone, you need a replacement."

"I don't need shit from you, Barrabas!" said the bandit.

"But your general does."

The bandit leader stood in silence for a moment, frowning deeply. His ugly face became even uglier as he tried urgently to think. After a long and evidently very painful moment, he called to one of his men and gave the order in Chinese to deliver a message to General Chien.

More long moments of waiting followed. The bandits gathered around the little band and laughed and spoke among themselves, eyeing Diana once in a while.

The messenger finally returned and whispered something into the ear of the bandit leader. The dirty fellow scowled. "It seems the general wants to talk to you, Barrabas. I will have to postpone your death for a while." He shrugged and looked resigned. "It will make it all the more fun."

They were made to stand there under heavy armed guard for more than an hour. They did not speak and the SOBs all did mind exercises to keep their cool. They knew this old trick. They were being forced to wait and made unable to relax so they would be nervous, tense and off their guard for the meeting with Chien.

Diana did very well under the circumstances. She, too, knew what the score was. She stood close to Barrabas for reassurance, forcing herself to keep calm, thinking about her eventual return to Rangoon and a hot bath, a good meal and sleep in a soft bed for about a month. She would be a heroine. She would get a raise. Maybe she would quit this business and become a schoolteacher.

Finally a man who was apparently a servant came out of the mansion and walked down the pathway to where Barrabas and his group were waiting. He looked directly at Barrabas. "The general will see you now. He will grant an audience only to Colonel Barrabas. The others will have to remain here."

Barrabas turned to his people and nodded reassuringly, then he turned around and followed the servant down the path and up the steps to the massive porch of the house. They disappeared inside, and the doors closed behind them.

Diana watched the big doors close behind Barrabas. She actually felt relieved that she wasn't going in there with him.

Billy reached up and placed a gentle hand on her shoulder. He leaned forward and spoke softly to her. "Don't worry, kid. It's in the bag now. The colonel will have us running this place in a few minutes."

Diana shuddered. She'd rather the colonel have them on a plane heading back to civilization!

BARRABAS WAS STOPPED just inside the door by a huge Tibetan with a DSh K-38 heavy SMG slung across his massive back.

"Xonn will take your weapons," explained the servant.

Barrabas had expected as much and gave up his M-16 and Browning HP. The guard took the guns and set them aside. The servant gave Barrabas a little nod and led him into the house proper.

The mansion appeared to be very opulently appointed. Plush carpets graced the floor and objets d'art adorned the rooms, all meticulously selected and coordinated. The furniture seemed to be the finest handcrafted work the world could provide.

The servant led Barrabas down a long, wide hallway. Xonn followed close behind. Barrabas looked into the massive rooms as they passed the doorways and knew that the man he had to deal with had amassed immense wealth.

They had walked almost to the end of the hall, when the servant turned and indicated with a bow that Barrabas should enter the room on their left. Barrabas walked through the door and the servant followed. Xonn continued to bring up the rear.

Entering the room was like going back to ancient China. Every detail echoed the era of the Ming dynasty. From the statues to the hanging silks, from the pottery and hand-painted urns to the gold dragons on the walls, every detail was perfect. The room was lit by lights shaped to resemble torches and candles.

But the surprising thing in the room was the man sitting on a massive chair against the far wall. Carved dragons seemed to hover above him on the wall panels, as if protecting their master. General Tai Ta Chien sat ramrod straight and definitely had the bearing of a man used to absolute obedience.

General Chien was certainly a remarkable individual, Barrabas noted as he approached the man. His head was shaved completely, and his long, thin mustache hung down well past his square jaw. Despite that affectation, he was dressed in a white silk suit and seemed somewhat out of place in the room's ornate, antique Oriental furnishings. Helping to restore the mood were two Chinese servant girls wearing embroidered silk robes. The lovely girls were sitting at the foot of their master. They belonged to Chien, beautiful objects that showed off another aspect of his incredible wealth.

The servant who had escorted Barrabas walked to the general's right and stood beside the throne. The Tibetan guard, still holding the submachine gun, took his place on the other side of the general. Barrabas stopped directly before Chien and gave him a solemn look.

"I've come to offer my services."

General Chien smiled. He took a deep, meaningful breath through his nose, then spoke softly and slowly in a deep voice, every syllable letting Barrabas know he was an extremely dangerous and powerful man.

"Colonel Nile Barrabas. Once with the U.S. Special Forces. Currently working as a mercenary."

"You've heard of me," stated Barrabas.

Chien laughed. "It would be impossible not to have heard of you, Colonel Barrabas. Ever since you came to Burma you have been making noise. You evidently think you are something special. You have come to take over the poppy trade."

"I figured I had the inside edge," said Barrabas. "I have an ex-DEA agent working with me and a fine team to back up my moves."

"Those three people outside?"

"That's all that's left of them. Your Captain Edmond and his assassins took care of the rest."

"And what has happened to Captain Edmond?" asked Chien.

"I killed him...as well as his team. That's why I'm here. I figured that with Edmond gone, you'd be needing another enforcer."

"And you have come to apply for the job."

"That's right."

"And what has happened to your vision of taking over the Indochinese drug business? Isn't working for me stepping down a bit?" asked Chien. His black eyes bored into the American's as if wanting to see his very thoughts, but Barrabas just shrugged.

"I had no idea you had such a well-organized operation, General. From all the reports I had before coming here, the Asian drug trade is in turmoil, ready for easy pickings to anybody with the know-how and a good team. I have the men, and my partner, Miss Simone, formerly of the Drug Enforcement Agency, has the know-how. Hell, I thought it would be easy."

"And what made Miss Simone leave DEA and join up with a free-lance adventurer?"

"Greed," said Barrabas.

General Chien smiled again. "Of course. An understandable emotion."

He sat in silence for a long moment, apparently considering Barrabas's offer. The scene froze, became like a still life in a painting of ancient China.

Chien finally spoke again. "You have a certain confidence, Colonel Barrabas, which is a trait I admire in a man. And it is true that with Edmond gone I will be needing another man to act as my enforcer. I am in a business where there is a great demand for strong enforcement practices."

"I can imagine," said Barrabas.

"You have an admirable reputation and appear to be a man who gets things done. You also seem to have a level head and know when to, shall I say, change the game of the cards."

"You ever hear the expression 'if you can't beat 'em, join 'em'?" asked Barrabas.

"Quite. Yes…it does seem appropriate." Chien sat in silence again for a moment, still pondering his options. He finally came to a conclusion. "Yes. I will need a good man to replace Edmond and you seem to have inherited the title. You and your followers could be the enforcement team I will need. I believe I shall let you try the job, at least for the present. How you handle the situations you face and your honor in serving me shall determine your staying in the position. Do you understand what I am telling you?"

"Yeah," said Barrabas. "Do it or lose it."

Chien chuckled. "Yes. Exactly. I think I like you, Colonel Barrabas. This may be the beginning of a very good relationship."

"I hope so."

"The wing of the house that used to belong to the unfortunate Captain Edmond is at your disposal. I believe you will find your accommodations satisfactory."

"I'm sure I will," said Barrabas. "Especially after living in the jungle the past few days."

Chien turned to the servant at his right. "Po, you shall escort Colonel Barrabas and his people to the south wing, where they shall take quarters."

Po bowed and indicated that Barrabas should go with him.

They turned to leave the incredible room and Chien called back to Barrabas. "Just one thing to remember, Colonel. Your service will mean much to me, but your life means nothing."

"I'll keep that in mind," said Barrabas, and he followed the obedient servant back into the hallway.

15

Edmond sat on the smooth surface of the wet stone and listened to the sounds of the firefight to the north. He figured it was either two rival drug armies or a band of poppy bandits caught by a patrol. He heard the two thumps and concussion explosions of the grenades and knew someone was playing this one for keeps. He scowled, telling himself to keep to the south and out of trouble, and he took another gnashing bite from the small carcass in his hand.

Edmond had been in the jungle for four days, finding his way back to Rutao from the Langtao swamps. Most of this time had been occupied with sheer survival. He had no weapon, no rations, no gear of any kind. He had started out wet, filthy and bone tired, and his condition deteriorated with every step he took.

Months of working as Chien's enforcer had familiarized him with the Kumon Range territory. He was able to use dead reckoning and steering marks to find his way east and to stay off the beaten paths, out of the way of the many roving patrols. His only aim was to get back to the Rutao estate and put together another team.

Then he would track down Barrabas and kill him.

Edmond tore off the last of the meat with his teeth and discarded the remains of the small jungle creature under the stone. He reached into the pockets of his torn fatigue trousers, pulled out a handful of wild tropical almonds and munched on them.

It was now very quiet to the north. The skirmish was over. One side would have won, and the dead of the losing band would be left on the jungle trail for the scavengers. There were winners and there were losers. It was all a part of the game of life and death.

Edmond was a survivor. He considered himself a winner. He had no doubt he would make it back to Chien's estate and put together another team. He had no doubt he would hunt for Barrabas, find him and kill him with his bare hands. Marshall Edmond was a positive thinker.

Edmond finished the nuts and used the back of his left hand to wipe his mouth and chin. He still had some gao beans, but decided to save them until he found water.

At the end of the war, when Edmond had been forced to flee from Saigon and disappear into the void of Indochina's underground, he had learned, out of necessity, all the lessons of survival. He had to escape from the advancing NVA and Khmer Rouge death squads. He had wandered the jungles, taking up with bands of mercenaries and expatriate bandits. He had started at the bottom and made his way up the echelon of underworld power until he was commanding his own gang in Bangkok. Edmond thought about it and grinned as he considered that, compared to those days, this little hike back to Rutao was a picnic.

It was time to move again. His next goal was to find water fresh and pure enough to drink. His final target was Rutao, and Edmond knew he was less than a day's journey away from the estate. He would find water, set his bearings and begin the last leg of his journey.

He laughed. The last march home would be the beginning of his next mission, a very personal mission. He visualized his immediate future. He would rest, eat, build up his strength, then assemble a new team of experts, men skilled in dealing death and with no consciences. They should be creatures of destruction...as he was. He was now one with the jungle, something possibly less than human. He knew what he had to accomplish to get his mind back, to regain control of his life.

He had to kill Barrabas.

It was more than an obsession. More than a goal to strive for. It was necessary for his sanity and his survival. He and Barrabas could not live in the same time and place together. He would send Colonel Nile Barrabas to the beyond.

Edmond's thoughts were only of survival and revenge. His mind was going fast, a casualty of his surroundings. He would live only to kill. He had become like a monster sprung from legend and haunting the jungle for victims.

Edmond got up from the stone and stretched, his lean body and hard muscles rippling. He flexed his muscles and felt powerful like an animal, while his mind fed on his hatred.

He started out again, heading a bit to the south to stay far away from the place where the firefight had occurred. He certainly didn't need the troubles that an armed patrol or roving jungle gang would cause him. He needed only water, then enough strength to make the final trek to Rutao.

He looked up at the sky through the jungle foliage. Yes, he would make it to Chien's estate before nightfall. He had enough of this day left to finish the trip.

With a new burst of energy from his deadly enthusiasm, Edmond bounded over a fallen rhododendron and set a steady pace toward the east.

LESS THAN A MILE to the north, the two Chinese squads had been cautiously approaching the gully where they had the bandits trapped, when they heard the unmistakably deadly double ping of the two grenades being released. The patrol commanders didn't even have enough time to scream before the two M-26s flew up from the ditch, one to the right, one to the left, and caught them. Nanos had timed it perfectly.

The grenades blew, and Nanos gave his men the command to follow through. They lurched up from the ditch, dirt and rubble raining down on them, and opened up on the stunned survivors of the explosions. When Nanos and the two Langtao warriors were finished sweeping the area with fire, there were no survivors. The two Chinese patrols had been devastated.

Their ears were ringing from the concussion of the two grenades going off so close. The smoke and cordite stench made them gag. They sat back in the ditch for a moment to allow the aftereffects of battle subside.

After resting a few moments, Nanos gave the order for his men to follow him out of the gully. They climbed out cautiously and surveyed the carnage.

"We do one hell of a job!" said Bo San, very self-impressed.

"We fix them good!" exclaimed Mai Su.

Nanos only cursed and shook his head. "Let's just make it a point not to get caught like this again."

The two Langtao natives nodded. Bo San felt a bit ashamed. He had failed at his task. He vowed to himself that he would not fail again.

"Okay," said Nanos, thinking about new business. "We lost some time. We have to get on the move again. The first thing we need to do is get away from this place in case there are any other patrols close enough to have heard the fight."

They moved due west for about an hour. When they came to another small clearing in the jungle, Nanos called a halt. "We have enough distance from the battle now. We need to get our bearings and advance with care again."

They rested, drinking some water and eating cold rice. After the short break, Nanos roused the men and gave new orders.

"Bo San, move ahead again to scout the terrain. I believe we need to veer a bit to the south. Mai Su, we will head cautiously toward the southwest until we find a trail you're familiar with.

"Yes, boss," said Mai Su. "That should not be far."

"Good. That's what I thought. But the important thing is not to get caught again. Bo San? You hear me?"

"Okay." The Burmese native gave Nanos his best contrite look.

"Good," said Nanos. "Then lets get moving. We still have a good deal of daylight left, and it's a long way to Nepal."

16

The room was bugged. It was the first thing Barrabas had checked for when they were left alone. The place was wired from top to bottom.

Barrabas signaled Diana, and she nodded her understanding. They would have to play up their cover at all times, even at night, alone in their room.

Apart from the many listening devices, the accommodations were fantastic. Their room was spacious, clean and nicely furnished in Oriental decor. The adjoining bath was huge, with marble sink, sunken tub and four full-length mirrors. Diana squealed with pleasure when she saw it.

After escorting Diana and Barrabas to their quarters, Po had shown them through the apartment quickly and left, bowing to them respectfully. Barrabas had closed the door behind the servant, and it was at that point that they had surveyed the place for bugs.

Only a few moments after his departure Po was back again, knocking softly on the door.

Barrabas opened the door and looked questioningly at him. "What is it?"

"Excuse me, sir. I shall not intrude again. The general wishes for your and the lady's company at supper. You will be in the dining quarters in two hours. I shall return at that time to escort you.''

Po bowed formally, turned and walked away down the hall. Barrabas closed the door again and turned and looked at Diana. "We've been commanded to appear at dinner in two hours.''

"I heard," she said, "but I don't care! I'm starved! I'm so sick of field rations...it will be wonderful to have a real meal.''

"I imagine you want to get cleaned up.''

"How did you guess, Nile? I mean, it's only been about eight days since I've had a real bath. And these clothes are growing on me—I'm going to have to scrape them off.''

"Fine...fine. Why don't you use the bathroom first.''

She gave him a wicked smile and walked over to the massive closets. When she saw the lush contents, she gasped and emitted another squeal of pleasure. Beautiful clothing hung on four racks; men's sport coats, suits from Hong Kong, casual attire, sports duds and bush outfits...dresses, kimonos, blouses and slacks. Most of the ladies' garments would fit her, Diana decided. She began going through the apparel like a girl in a department store with her first charge card.

"That Captain Edmond had some taste!" she exclaimed, pulling out a colorful dress. It seemed to be of the finest silk. Diana held it up to take a good look at it. "Maybe I'll wear this to dinner.''

Barrabas began going through his gear. His weapons had not been returned to him. Diana's gun had also been taken away from her upon entering the house. Billy and Hayes were staying in one of the team houses. They were able to keep their weapons and gear with them. Like all the bandits and soldiers on the premises, they would be allowed to be armed.

Po had assumed that Diana was with Barrabas, and that earned her the right to stay with him inside the mansion. Otherwise she would have been living in one of the team houses, constantly warding off advances.

She had no idea how they would manage to remain alive, but the many scares she had had recently had taught her to start to at least try taking things as they came. So she took the Oriental dress into the bathroom and closed the door behind her. Barrabas sat on the bed, going over his gear, and heard her moving about, running water.

She was in there for over an hour. When she finally opened the door and emerged, it was to admit a totally new Diana Simone into the room. He stared briefly at the transformation. It was as if she had undergone a metamorphosis in the bath...a dirty worm becoming a beautiful, colorful butterfly.

Diana's long black hair was brushed, pulled back and tied at her nape and it flowed down her supple back. Her face glowed under a small amount of makeup and as an aftereffect of a lot of scrubbing. The jungle muck was gone, and the only thing that showed was a pretty woman. The dress fit her closely, and a slit up the side revealed a good deal of leg.

She knew she looked like a Hong Kong pleasure girl, but she didn't mind. It was, in fact, the effect she had worked for and just another part of the game.

After a long moment filled with meaningful silence, Diana asked the crucial question. "Well, how do I look?"

"You look fine," said Barrabas, shrugging, then he turned and pulled a pair of slacks and a sport shirt out of the closet and disappeared into the bathroom.

WHEN PO RETURNED, Barrabas and Diana were ready and waiting for him. Po led them down the long hallway and into the center of the mansion proper, where the huge dining room was located.

General Chien was sitting at the massive-looking dining table and did not stand as Barrabas and Diana were escorted into the room by Po and shown to seats at the general's right. There would be only the three of them at dinner that evening, though there was room enough for about twenty more at the table.

Barrabas and Diana took their places, and Po bowed to Chien and left the dining room. A servant girl immediately served them a chilled white wine. No doubt they would have to sit through a meal with many courses.

Chien looked over at Diana and gave her a smile that was unfathomable. "I have heard you made a shrewd career move," he said appraisingly.

Diana smiled back, trying to put a gleam of greed into her eyes. "Yes, General. I am sure it will be the right choice." She turned in her leather chair and gave Barrabas a quick look. He didn't notice. He was tasting his wine with a wry expression.

Chien noticed the look and spoke to Diana reassuringly. "Mercenaries try to act devil-may-care, but always come across as crude."

"Oh, I agree!" said Diana, giving an honest smile.

The servant girl came back into the dining room with three steaming bowls of vegetable soup. As she set them before the guests, Chien spoke. "The contents of the soup are all fresh, grown in my gardens on my estate. All the food I eat is pure and from my land. The game meat, poultry and fish are all from the surrounding bush. Captain Edmond often liked to hunt for food when he wasn't hunting men for me. It kept him in form. Possibly you would enjoy joining in on one of the hunting parties, Colonel Barrabas."

"I guess it beats doing the dishes."

Chien cackled again. "Oh, Colonel...you try so hard to appear flippant. You missed your calling. You should have been an actor instead of a soldier."

Barrabas shrugged and took another sip of the wine, hoping that the act was coming off. It wasn't. Chien's trust for them was nil.

Diana tasted the soup. "Mmm—General, this is delicious!"

Chien smiled. "Thank you, Diana. May I call you 'Diana'?"

"Of course."

"You are such a lovely woman. It is unfortunate that you belong to Colonel Barrabas."

Diana gave Chien a stern look. "I don't belong to anybody, General."

"Of course." He gave her a little bow. "Not even the DEA. You have proven your independence by re-

signing your position and joining up with Colonel
Barrabas. It is such a shame in a way. Particularly now
that I have seen how beautiful you are. Your Eurasian radiance is truly stunning. You fit the code name
of Dragon Lady perfectly."

"That was only a term some of my contacts used,
General...not a code name. It was derived from a
comic-strip character, a Eurasian heroine with a reputation for being sneaky."

"And was that a description of you, Diana?" asked
General Chien.

"Let's just say I wasn't very fond of the nick-
name."

Another cackle came out of Chien. He turned to eat
his soup in silence. Barrabas was getting edgy and tried
to keep his mind clear so his concern wouldn't show.
The general was no fool.

The general swallowed, used his napkin to wipe his
mustache and looked back up at his guests. "Let me
just say that I find it hard to believe that such a dedicated agent of drug enforcement would turn...bad—
I believe that is the expression I want."

Diana sighed and looked directly at him. "I just got
damned tired of being on the short end of things all
the time. I worked myself to death, and for what? I
just want to enjoy a little of the good life, and I want
the beautiful things that will be a proper setting for
my...looks," she finished modestly.

Barrabas was impressed. She was putting on a good
act. Still, General Chien wasn't about to trust them,
and they would have to play it to the hilt.

Chien gave Diana a little bow. "I understand your feelings perfectly."

"Isn't that why you left the Chinese army, General? So you could have a proper showcase for your style and talents?" Diana was being bold.

"Let me say those were certainly some of the reasons," said Chien.

The servant girl returned to take the soup bowls away. Two others followed her into the dining hall to serve fresh trout with lemon wedges, as well as meats beautifully presented on platters. Soon there was a rich array of succulent food before them. Bowls of rice were placed before the guests, a mixture of wild grains and brown with slivered tropical almonds on top. More wine was made available, as well as a chilled pitcher of spring water.

"This looks wonderful!" said Diana, beaming at the food. She was ravished after days of eating field rations and felt true enthusiasm about a good meal.

Though Diana did justice to the dinner, and Barrabas ate sparingly, General Chien worked his way through small amounts at a time, talking most of the while.

"Let's say the real reason I resigned my commission in the army was because of my mixed feelings about the politics of modern China. I do not like what has happened to my country. I am a man from the old way, a believer in the true China. You must be able to relate to my feelings, Colonel. You left your army for much the same reason, did you not?"

Barrabas gave him a nod, but did not comment. He wanted the general to keep talking.

"I do not like Communism," Chien continued. "It has destroyed our nation. It has ruined the values of true China. I served the Communist military because I was a born soldier and a leader of China's people. It was my born purpose... but my calling is to become a true leader. More than a warlord. More than even an emperor. I shall be China's savior!"

Barrabas was pretending to divide his attention between his host and the food, but his mind was concentrating fully on what Chien was telling him. This wasn't what he had expected. He always thought Chien was a retired general who'd sought power and wealth in Southeast Asia's massive drug business. He figured Chien's dreams of leadership had ended with an organized drug empire... a cartel of land barons and poppy warlords who could form their own little empire in Indochina and rule the underworld of drugs.

Evidently Chien's visions of power were much grander. As Chien talked, Barrabas formed the picture of a man with ideas and dreams of military expansion among the Indochinese states and lesser nations; of expansion and subversion throughout China, fueled by the millions of dollars from his drug trade. Chien was a powerful arms dealer, too, stockpiling massive caches of weapons for the eventual revolution. His private armies, as well as those of the other warlords in the cartel, would be the foundation of the new military body. The bands of mercenaries, bandits, pirates and native warriors were his recruits, men to be turned into soldiers for his cause.

The whole thing was incredible, and Barrabas hadn't been expecting it. He began to have mixed feelings about Chien. The man wanted to overthrow the Chinese Communist government and rebuild China. Chien was certainly crazy and his methods were amoral to the point of being evil, but there was something to be said for his ultimate goal.

"I shall not see the final outcome of my plans in my lifetime," said Chien. "Possibly my son will not be the one to carry out the final act. It may be my grandson...but there will be an Emperor Chien to rule over China at a new time!"

They finished supper, and the servant girls returned to remove the plates and bowls. As the girls worked, Barrabas sat back in his chair and sipped water. He didn't want to show too much interest in Chien. He had to keep up the act of a mercenary interested only in work for pay.

"And now I have a special treat for you," said Chien. He nodded to the head servant girl. She bowed and quickly left the room.

She came back in a moment, carrying a tray with two frosty glasses of beer. It was the same local brand they had been served in the tavern in Rutao.

"This is a beverage you enjoy," Chien said as the girl placed the drinks in front of the guests. "It is what you ordered upon your visit to the Viper's Hole Tavern."

Barrabas gave Chien a rare smile. "I'm impressed."

"I know all that happens in my empire," stated Chien, playing his role of ruler to the hilt.

Diana just stared at the glass of beer. She was suddenly very nervous, and reminded herself where she was and what she was doing. Mistakes would be deadly. She had to concentrate to be able to play out their dangerous game.

Barrabas picked up the mug and took a long swallow of the cold brew. "Ah, good, General. That's real good."

"I'm very happy you are enjoying it, Colonel Barrabas. And how about you, Diana? Did the meal please you?"

"Yes, it was excellent." There wasn't a lot of enthusiasm in her tone.

"Good, good." The general turned to the servant girl and nodded. He received another bow and the girl rushed from the room. "And now I have a very, very special treat for dessert. In fact, this will be the most remembered portion of the meal."

The girl returned in a moment with a huge round silver platter with a snug-fitting cover. The servant held the platter over the table and placed her hand on the handle of the lid. She waited, looking at Chien to give her the command to serve the dessert.

"One of my men was recently discovered to be a traitor," said Chien. "He was selling some of my ideas and plans to a rival tribe of Lahs. Our dessert this evening shall be a lesson in how I deal with traitors."

He gave the girl the nod she was waiting for and she immediately removed the lid from the platter.

Diana gasped and turned very white. She averted her face and buried it against Barrabas's strong shoulder.

On the platter were the insides of the traitor. He had been slit open and disemboweled, and his organs had been poured onto the serving dish.

General Chien assumed a grave expression. "You see? This is what happens to traitors, liars and sneaks. Do you see it, Diana? Why don't you take another good look?"

Diana felt she was going to be sick. Barrabas looked challengingly at Chien. "Take that mess out of here!" Barrabas's cold eyes became slits of deadly meaning. His glare reached out and grabbed at Chien, filled with certain danger. "Get it the hell away from here!"

General Chien just stared back at Barrabas, obviously having made the point that he would do the same to them, if necessary.

As Barrabas stood to leave the table, bringing Diana to her feet, something red and wet splashed onto the tablecloth.

17

Marshall Edmond didn't want to spend another night in the jungle. He was tired of the insects, the ants as big as bullets, biting him and feeding on him as he tried to sleep. He didn't want to hear the sounds of nocturnal kills, the weeps of dying animals and pathetic cries of pain and death that filled the Burmese night. He wanted to spend this night in his apartment, in his bed, not half resting in the muck while always listening, waiting for the snakes or roving bandits.

Edmond was so close to the estate that he could sense it—almost feel it, smell it! In a few hours he could clean up and eat real food. And then there would be his woman.

He crouched in the bush and his nerves felt as though they were being torn from his flesh. He beat the mossy ground with a fist, giving vent to his rage and frustration. He was so close to climbing out of the muck. So close! He silently cursed his bad luck...and cursed the Burmese gods for the thousandth time for their mean sense of humor.

There was movement on the trail in front of him. It was the distinct sound of human footsteps. They were muffled, and that could signal natives or a well-trained

Burmese government patrol. He crouched lower, listening with acute attention, his senses honed by his days in the jungle. They were still too far away for him to tell who they were. The only thing Edmond knew for sure was that they meant trouble.

He was just too close now to be captured or killed....

It had taken him much longer than he had expected to locate fresh drinking water. He had wasted almost two hours searching for a stream or spring he could drink from. By the time he found the spring bubbling into the pond, he was off his trail and needed to rest and get his bearings again.

Now dark was quickly approaching. The Indochinese nightfall came suddenly and quickly. He was close to being forced to spend yet another night in the jungle, concentrating on survival. He had to make quick time...but now he was trapped.

Survival had been his whole life for the past five days...his whole existence. Every move he made, every motion produced by his body, every thought and idea and breath was a concentrated effort to survive.

And now he was so close...the estate was a matter of hours away...and he was cornered. Trapped like the animal he had become.

The men on the trail were coming closer. Jungle men on the hunt. Dangerous men!

Edmond crouched lower, becoming as though one with the earth. He willed himself to relax, controlling his body functions. He breathed slowly through his nose. He squinted to peer through the brush and the twilight. He cocked his head and listened, reaching out

with his senses like a frightened beast. He hated what
he had become.

The men came closer, moving at a steady pace on
the winding trail. Good. They would pass soon. He
stopped breathing and lowered his head, waiting for
them to move by.

Then the worst possible thing happened. They
stopped. They were directly in front of him, five or six
of them, and they stopped. They knew he was there....

He listened as they spoke softly in one of the many
Burmese native dialects. They were from a local tribe.
They knew their territory... they were one with the
land. They would know when an animal was hiding,
trapped...and they would always be looking for food.

He listened. They continued to speak and he could
understand some of what they were saying. They were
looking for him! They had been tracking him! And
they knew that they had him....

He did not want to die now...here...he had a
mission in his life!

They were leaving the trail, coming into the brush
toward him. He lifted his head, squinting to see them.

Foliage parted. He saw the spears and the M-1 rifle.
He looked up higher, into the white eyes and painted
faces. He had no strength. He knew he couldn't fight.
One of them laughed, showing flashing teeth.

"Goddam that Nile Barrabas to hell!" Edmond
exploded, and they reached for him.

18

Billy Starfoot II moved along the jungle path with the ease and certainty of his full-blooded Osage heritage. The many years he'd spent as a professional soldier didn't hurt, either, and he had patrolled a lot of wild, untamed places. He served as the point man with absolute confidence, almost flowing through the bush in his search for the bandit camp.

Barrabas and Hayes were close behind, moving a bit slower, covering the rear while assisting in the terrain search. It was their third little outing for General Chien in as many days, hunting rival bandit gangs, poachers and intruders on his precious land.

They had been living on Chien's estate for four days, keeping up their cover as his enforcement team. So far the job had been a breeze. Their assignments had been to get rid of intruders on the general's very private property. It was proving to be nothing difficult or anything that would conflict with their true purpose for being there.

The afternoon heat was oppressive. Barrabas called a break. Billy stopped and waited for his two comrades to catch up to him.

The three men sat on a log and drank deeply from their canteens. The cold spring water tasted good.

Hayes wiped the sweat away from his brow and looked at Barrabas. "How long before Nanos should return with the cavalry, Colonel?"

Barrabas sat in silence for a moment, thinking before he answered. He didn't like dealing with uncertainties in the field, but in this case he had no options.

"He could be back by tomorrow. I expect it will be two days, though, and...well, if he isn't back by the end of the third, we'll go to Plan B."

Plan B meant that Nanos didn't make it to Nepal. If he didn't return in the given time, Barrabas and his team would go out on another job for Chien and disappear into the bush. They would make their way to Nepal and return with the strike force necessary to wipe Chien and his estate off the face of the Earth.

The only problem was Diana. She wasn't allowed to go out on assignments with the SOBs. Chien kept her back at the house, knowing this would force Barrabas and his men to return.

They wouldn't leave her.

Barrabas had been pondering the dilemma for the past three days. It was good to be away from the estate, out in the field with his men, where it was safe to talk. They had to keep up their act, never let down their guard every minute they were at Chien's estate. Barrabas and Diana even had to keep up the show when they were alone in their room.

They had found something of a solution though. They could go into the bathroom, run the shower and, under the sound of the rushing water, speak softly. They took a lot of showers, but at least Diana was kept informed of his plans.

And he assured Diana in no uncertain terms that he would not leave her behind if worse came to worse.

Now he needed another plan...or at least a modified Plan B that would include Diana's escape. He sat on the log and thought about it as he rested, but a feasible solution just wouldn't come. Their only hope now was that Nanos and the Langtao warriors would make it to Nepal and return with Colonel Calvert and the First Battalion.

Still, Barrabas didn't like not having a workable alternative. If only they didn't have the DEA agent to worry about....

Barrabas took another swallow of water and put the canteen back on his webbing. He stood and his men followed suit.

No use worrying about the future now. They had a job to do.

It took them less than an hour to locate the bandit camp. Billy spotted it first as he moved ahead on the point again. He motioned to the others to halt, then to advance slowly.

Barrabas and Hayes approached Billy with caution, not making a sound. They moved to his side and peered through the foliage. They had found their target.

There were only five of them, the smallest band they had faced yet in their police work for Chien. The others had been easy to deal with; a few warning shots and stern words, then run them off the land. There had been no conflict. None of the other intruders had argued with Barrabas and his men, apart from a few curses in Burmese thrown in for good measure.

This little group had set up a makeshift camp in the northern part of the Chien's property. They were transporters of contraband from China who took their wares to the black markets in India. They were simple dealers and thieves, a tiny part of the vast network of Asian criminals. They wouldn't want trouble.

Barrabas looked at the men in the little camp. This all seemed so pointless. These guys were doing nothing but trying to make a living in the easiest field in this part of the world. Their only crime against General Chien was trespassing. Yet he wanted them hunted down and eliminated. Barrabas had to wonder how many men like these Edmond had tracked down and killed in cold blood.

Barrabas turned to his men and spoke in a whisper. "Okay. Let's let them know we're here. A few shots in the air should do it."

The two SOBs nodded at their leader and fired three rounds each from their M-16s. The five bandits simultaneously jumped, glanced around nervously and reached for their weapons.

The shots from the M-16s were still ringing when Barrabas shouted into the camp. He hoped the bandits spoke English, but if they didn't, his tone would tell them he was there on serious business.

"Drop the guns! Just stay where you are! You are covered! If you move, we will kill you!"

He let them see he was armed and serious, aiming the M-16 into the center of the camp, at the fire where the men had been cooking a meal.

"Put down the guns! Now! We are coming into your camp!"

Barrabas had just started to move forward, when the game unexpectedly changed. One of the bandits lifted his M-1 and fired at him. The merc leader cursed and dashed for cover as the rounds tore through the foliage above him.

Billy and Hayes both opened up at the same time on the furious thief. Their shots caught him in the chest, throwing him back into the dirt. He was able to squeeze one last shot out of his rifle with a reflex action, and it was the last act he would perform in this world.

Billy and Hayes continued aiming into the camp, but now they were pointing their weapons directly at the four remaining bandits. The men looked nervous and were casting scared glances at their fallen comrade. They were also talking, attempting to make something understood.

Barrabas lifted his head and looked at the bandit camp. The four remaining men didn't appear to have a lot of fight left in them, but they were still clutching their automatic weapons. Men in their trade were always armed to the teeth.

"Drop the guns!" Barrabas was still angry and he got off two more warning shots into the fire, scattering sparks and flaming twigs. "Get my meaning?"

The four bandits threw down their weapons and lifted their arms above their heads.

Barrabas sighed, then stepped over the foliage he had been using for cover and walked toward the camp. Billy and Hayes followed behind, aiming their M-16s at the hapless men.

Barrabas slung his weapon over his shoulder before picking up the four guns from where the bandits had dropped them and handing them to his men. He walked over and looked down at the dead thief, whose blood was seeping into the dirt in a steady stream.

Barrabas turned to the other bandits, their hands still in the air. "Any of you speak English?"

"I speak some," said one of the bandits. He was the fellow who looked the most nervous. He was certain that he was going to die and was actually shaking in his terror.

Barrabas stared at him and spoke slowly. "You are trespassing. This land belongs to General Chien, a crude and extremely stupid bastard. He does not want you on his land. Do you understand what I am telling you?"

The nervous bandit nodded quickly. "Yes, yes! General Chien is a bastard." The man knew what this strange soldier was saying, but he couldn't believe it. Didn't he work for General Chien? Hadn't he been sent to hunt and kill them? He had heard the warnings about an American killer who protected Chien's land ruthlessly...but this odd man didn't fit the description.

"That is correct," said Barrabas. "So this mean mother doesn't want you on his crummy and worthless land. He has sent us to run you off."

"Okay!" agreed the bandit. "We go now...."

"First you can bury your comrade."

"Oh...that not necessary. It does not matter to him anymore."

"You'll bury him and then we'll escort you off the general's land," stated Barrabas, and the subject was closed.

The bandit grinned widely. Then turned and spoke hurriedly to his three partners. After all-around nods of approval they enthusiastically began to prepare a grave.

Barrabas leaned against a tree and lit a cigar, watching the four bandits work. The two SOBs were keeping them covered for good measure.

Barrabas blew a stream of smoke into the still, humid air, thinking that he wouldn't be able to continue with this kind of nonsense for long. He seriously hoped Nanos was making good time on the trail. Barrabas just wanted to get on with his real mission before he lost his self-respect.

WATER WAS RUNNING. Diana was filling the tub for her nightly bath. She also had the water flowing in the sink, pretending to wash the makeup from her face before she bathed. Barrabas was running the water in the shower stall.

"It should sound like Niagara Falls," said Diana.

"We can't be too careful," said Barrabas. He had just returned from his assignment in the bush. He and his two men had reported to Chien and given him a quick briefing on the success of their mission. Barrabas hadn't gone into detail on exactly how they had eliminated the problem, only that the little bandit gang wouldn't trespass on Chien's precious land anymore.

General Chien told the men he was happy with their success and dismissed them for the remainder of the evening. Barrabas had gone to his room, where Diana was waiting.

"Hi, babe. Tough day, and I'm ready for something relaxing." He spoke to keep up their cover, but his eyes and expression told her a different story. He indicated the bath with a nod, and she returned his signal. It was time to talk.

"Let's get cleaned up," said Diana, also playing the role. "Then I'll bet we can come up with something even more relaxing."

They had entered the bath together and turned on all the water faucets.

"I'm getting nervous, Nile," said Diana, speaking as softly as possible. "You know what's happening tomorrow."

"Yeah. The big meeting of the cartel. The Seven will start gathering in the morning."

"That's right, and some of those guys really don't like me. I've given them a lot of grief over the years."

"I'm not exactly on their top ten buddy list."

"And now we're supposed to convince them that we want to be pals and work with them? I really don't know if we can pull it off."

Barrabas shrugged. "We'll do the best we can. Anyway, Nanos is due back at any time. Our main concern is to be ready for him and the strike."

"Well, you've spent enough time wandering around and getting the layout of the place. If we're not ready now, we'll never be."

"We're ready," stated Barrabas.

Diana thought in silence for a moment. Barrabas knew what her next question would be.

"Have you thought about what we're going to do if Nanos doesn't return? I mean, if he didn't make it to Nepal?"

"I've thought about it," said Barrabas. The remark was followed by a long silence.

Diana looked at him questioningly.

"I'm still thinking."

Diana nodded solemnly. "Everything depends on Nanos's making it to Nepal. We're stuck in a house full of Indochina's most notorious drug warlords and kingpins, and our one chance to get out is coming from the outside!"

"You'll be the first to know if I come up with an alternative," said Barrabas.

"My God, Barrabas, I can't believe I let you get me into this!"

He shrugged again. "I gave you a number of chances to bow out and go back home. You stuck with it. You'll be proud of yourself when it's over."

"Wonderful! As I'm being sliced open by one of Chien's goons I can be saying to myself, 'I didn't quit...I can be proud!' That's great!" She forced herself to take a deep breath to regain her composure.

Barrabas shrugged and said, "Nanos is a damned fine man. He won't let us down."

"I sure hope you're right. So...what happens next?"

Barrabas started taking off his fatigue shirt. He was filthy and tired from the trek through Chien's land. And he would need his rest for the next day.

"I'm going to take my shower," he told Diana. "Then I'm going to get a good night's sleep. I suggest you do the same. Tomorrow could be a bitch."

"Tell me about it."

She turned off the water in the tub and sink and left the bath. As she closed the door behind her, she heard Barrabas humming in the shower.

She sighed and stood there for a moment, leaning against the door. Her nerves were just too jumpy to allow her a good rest. She wanted to run away from the place. It was ironic that she was afraid she was going to die and Barrabas was humming in the shower.

19

The road was filled with potholes and deep ruts. Nanos clutched the steering wheel of the truck, fighting to keep it straight while maintaining the quick pace he had set. On the bench seat next to him, the two Langtao natives bounced around and grunted with each jarring thump.

They had been driving all night, trying to make better time now that they were inside India. Nanos and his men had made it to the Pangsau Pass before the end of their third day out. There had been no further incidents since the battle with the Chinese patrols, apart from a few times they had had to hole up to avoid the roving bandit caravans and gangs.

After going through the simple checkpoint at the Pangsau Pass and entering India, Nanos had walked directly into Ledo, where he had bought an Army-surplus pickup truck with the expense money Barrabas had given him. Nanos hadn't bartered for the vehicle. The Indian salesman had quoted a price and Nanos had paid cash. He had made the salesman's day. It had been the first sale the man had had in more than two weeks.

The three warriors had stripped off their gear and stored it in the back of the truck, then climbed into the cab. The two natives had grinned. It was a real outing for them. A real treat!

Nanos had quickly scanned his map and shifted the truck into gear. The engine was in good shape and the body was sturdy. The motor purred into life and ran smoothly. Nanos drove out of Ledo and met the roughly paved road that would take them most of the way across the eastern handle of India.

They drove the entire fourth day and night, eating the remainder of their field rations and drinking from their canteens. They stopped only for rest breaks, stretching the tightness out of the lower backs and relieving themselves. The shocks on the truck were in extremely poor condition, and their kidneys were battered from the bouncing and tossing around the men took from the fast pace Nanos set. A few discomforts didn't matter, though, when the very lives of Colonel Barrabas and the team were at stake.

By the middle of the night they were just south of Bhutan, heading west at a good clip toward the border of Nepal. Nanos was feeling good. He was very proud of himself. He was making even better time than he had expected, despite the fight with the Chinese soldiers and the few other minor setbacks. He would make the border of Nepal by early morning and make contact with Colonel Calvert at the battalion post by midmorning. Then there would be a quick briefing and prep for the strike, and they would be back to Rutao and Chien's estate before nightfall.

Nanos was feeling confident. Everything was going right for once. Everything was falling into place. Some of their missions in the past had gone to hell about this point, but he had made it to India and all enemy territory was behind. It was a simple cross-country drive from here.

He was dead tired, but he couldn't think about it. The two Langtao natives took naps in the seat next to him. They shifted their weapons and the bit of gear they had kept on them around and slept fitfully. It was virtually impossible to relax in the bouncing truck, but they were tired enough to get a little rest.

Nanos knew they would need it. They both planned on following the mission through to the finish. Both warriors planned on going back with Nanos and Colonel Calvert's men to hit Chien's estate. Nanos didn't argue with them. They had done a tremendous job for him and deserved to be in on the finish. They were good soldiers.

Nanos rubbed his eyes and tried to focus better, to concentrate fully on the twisting road in front of him. He could rest on the trip back to Rutao. It would take the choppers nine or ten hours to reach northern Burma, enough time for Nanos to catch some good sleep and be alert to guide the strike force into Chien's estate.

It was all going by the numbers at this point. The colonel would be expecting them tomorrow and Nanos would arrive right on time with the cavalry! Just like in the movies! Just the way a mission is supposed to run. He was feeling the joy of overconfidence, when things started to deteriorate.

First there was the tree across the road. Nanos pulled the truck to a stop with a heartfelt curse. He woke up his two partners and it took them the better part of an hour to remove the oak so they could continue their drive.

Next one of the caps on a reserve tank of gas came off and a good portion of their fuel spilled into the bed of the truck, soaking the gear. Nanos immediately pulled the truck over to the side of the road and stopped when he saw the problem. Their equipment would dry out, but now Nanos didn't know if they had enough fuel left to make the remainder of the trip. They would have to keep their eyes open for a source of fuel.

Then there was the trouble from Tibet.

A group of Tibetan revolutionaries seeking independence from China had attacked a police station in Lhasa, killing most of the officers on duty and doing a tremendous amount of damage. They had burned the building, overturned police vehicles and cut the power to the station, as well as to all the surrounding buildings. Then they had fled south into India in a small convoy of trucks.

Chinese authorities were immediately notified of the situation. A patrol was sent out from Kula Kangri to cross the border into India and hunt for the fleeing revolutionaries. All major roads and border towns were being checked thoroughly.

When Nanos saw the roadblock at Sikkim, he knew they were in trouble. They were armed to the teeth and caught dead on the road. He had to make a decision: to try to fight his way through, or to turn and run.

Nanos decided to go on . . . and fight.

He pulled up to the roadblock and stopped at the command of the Chinese soldier. When the man approached the truck with a high-beamed flashlight, Nanos and the two natives did the best they could to hide their weapons and ammo pouches. It didn't work.

The soldier took one good look into the truck cab and saw the weapons. He began shouting in Chinese, and three others soldiers started trotting toward the truck. Nanos and his men were going to be arrested . . . no questions asked.

Nanos cursed. He brought his M-16 up on his lap and shot the hat off the Chinese soldier. The man screamed and dropped down to the ground, next to the truck, fumbling for his gun. Nanos floored the gas pedal and smashed through the feeble roadblock.

Chinese soldiers began firing at the racing truck. The back window was blown to hell, glass spraying over the Langtao warriors. They ducked in their seats, but not before Bo San took a round in the back of the skull. His face blew apart as the slug came out and blood and brains splashed on the truck's dashboard. He died instantly.

Mai Sui cried out with grief. He was sitting between Nanos and the body of Bo San. His friend's corpse bounced on the seat and fell across his lap.

"Get rid of it, Mai! Get rid of the body!" Nanos clutched the wheel and fought to keep the truck on the road. They were hitting the bumps and chuck holes with tremendous force, and the Greek didn't know how long the shocks could last. He also realized he was using a hell of a lot of their precious remaining fuel.

But he had no choice. The Chinese were coming after them in two jeeps...two well-maintained jeeps with excellent shocks and plenty of fuel! Nanos glanced at the reflection of the dual set of headlights in his rearview mirror and gave off a heartfelt curse.

Mai Su was quickly over his shock. His instinct to survive took over. They needed to get rid of excess weight and he needed room to maneuver and fight if that became necessary. Bo San's body would have to go.

Mai Su reached across the corpse and grabbed the door handle of the truck. The vehicle hit a rut and bounced, forcing him to lose his grip. He lurched once more, grabbed the door handle again and turned it. Then he gave a shove, and the body of Bo San rolled out. Mai Su saw his friend hit the gravel, bounce and roll away. He gave off another little cry of grief and pulled the truck door shut again. Then he turned to Nanos, his sorrow gone, and let the Greek know with a nod that he was ready to survive.

Alex Nanos gave the brave warrior a grin...his best. He was a good soldier. "We're gonna make it, Mai. Just hang on!"

The Langtao native tried to smile. He gave Nanos a salute.

The pursuing jeeps were gaining quickly. Nanos watched them in the mirrors. He kicked on the accelerator, punched the wheel with his fist and cursed at the truck to make it go faster. That didn't work. The battered vehicle was no match for the Chinese army jeeps.

When Nanos had purchased the truck he hadn't planned on a high-speed chase across India. All he'd needed was an affordable vehicle to take them to the

Nepalese border. But now the game had turned ... as it so often did on a mission. They were no longer driving to a rendezvous point; they were racing for their lives!

The Chinese pulled close enough to begin shooting at their truck. Rounds hit the bed and the roof of the cab. Mai Su ducked as low on the seat as he could. He cried out in terror as a slug whizzed over his head and tore into the glove box.

A round caught Nanos in the right arm. It became useless. He grabbed the wheel with all the strength and force he had in his left arm, fighting desperately now just to keep the vehicle on the road. He wanted to clutch his wound—it felt as if his entire arm were on fire—but he couldn't. He had to ignore the pain, concentrate on driving the truck ... on surviving.

He didn't know how far they went. His vision was starting to blur. He was functioning in a daze. He just held the wheel with his good hand and pushed the pedal to the floor with his right foot, squinting through the broken windshield in an effort to see the dark road in front of them.

He was starting to black out. He cursed again, gave his head a shake, trying to clear his vision. He sensed one of the jeeps gaining, overtaking them on the right. Mai Sui was pointing his rifle out the side window, shooting at the jeep. Rounds from the Chinese weapons were hitting the door of the truck, their slaps echoing in Nanos's head like thunder.

His vision was getting dimmer. He was about to lose all control. Mai Su kept on blasting at the Chinese, and Nanos heard wild screams and felt the jarring crash as the jeep went out of control on the right, the driver dead across the wheel. Then Nanos lost it. The truck started to swerve madly, and the jeep behind them rammed into their rear. Nanos pushed his entire body against the steering wheel, trying to get some control.

He couldn't hold on. The truck went off the road, tipped over and rolled twice. Nanos bashed his head on the roof of the cab. Fighting off the dizziness he tried to stand up, but realized he was confined. The truck had come to rest on its wheels, upright. It had stalled, but he couldn't relate to that. He was still pressing on the accelerator, trying to drive away.

The jeep was pulling up on his side of the truck, the high beams flooding them with stinging light, and Mai Su was crawling over him, shooting out the window. The last thing Nanos was aware of before he lost his delicate hold on reality was the smell of gas. The odor saturated the air in the cab and Nanos knew they were about to explode. He told himself that it was a dumb but glorious way to die.

20

The ceiling fan turned at a slow, steady pace, drawing some of the thick, humid air up from within the little office. The blades caught the late-afternoon sunshine, and orange lights danced inside the room like a light-effects show at a rock concert.

Colonel Jonathan Calvert of the First Battalion 7th Gurkha Rifles in Nepal sat back in his chair and looked at the woman sitting on the opposite side of his small, cluttered desk. She was extremely attractive, with black eyes, dark hair and an intriguing, brooding expression. The black combat suit she wore was tailored to fit her fine, strong body, and Calvert thought she was the very last person he would have picked as liaison agent on a special warfare mission.

"Will you be leaving in the morning?" asked the colonel.

"No," stated the woman.

Calvert sighed for dramatic effect and leaned on his desk, barely able to find a clear place to put his elbows. "I'm afraid that word from your Colonel Barrabas is long overdue. The contact should have been made by today. It appears that he is lost.'

"No," the woman said again. "Not the colonel. I'll wait."

Calvert sat back in his chair again. It gave off a loud creak with his shifting weight. He took a dingy towel off the corner of the desk and wiped the flowing sweat from his brow.

He didn't know how to deal with the woman's stubborn persistence. He had other matters to attend to and couldn't wait any longer for word from the lost team. It wasn't the first failed mission that he had seen, and it wouldn't be the last.

Nile Barrabas had contacted Calvert more than a week ago, informing him of the plan. He was leading a team of special warfare agents on a search-and-destroy mission into northern Burma and the Golden Triangle regions. They would be looking for the jungle headquarters of the drug cartel. When they found it—if they found it—they would make contact with Colonel Calvert and his battalion of Gurkhas and the two groups would conduct a joint strike against the cartel.

The plan appealed to Calvert. The cartel was comprised of many a criminal warlord he and his men had been trying to put out of business for years. A hit on the entire cartel would be like killing many birds with one stone. He had assured Barrabas that his battalion would be ready, willing and extremely able to assist in the strike.

But Calvert also knew it wasn't as easy as Barrabas made it sound. The territory they were going into was a virtual war zone, filled with bandits, drug mercenaries, native tribes ruthlessly dealing in raw opium and numerous roving Asian criminal gangs. It was also pure wild bush, with the hazards of jungles, swamps, mountains and savage beasts. The team he was taking out on this mission would be up against very high odds.

Calvert had worked briefly with Barrabas in the past on training missions in India and Nepal. The British colonel had to admit that he respected Barrabas's talents as a soldier.

Evidently Barrabas and his team were now on a covert assignment for one of the U.S. secret agencies operating in the district. Calvert thought it was most likely the DEA, though he didn't know for sure. Nevertheless the mission was an honorable one, very ambitious, and its successful outcome would certainly be a boon to law enforcement agencies in both Near and Far Eastern parts of Asia.

Calvert had hoped against hope that it would turn out well.

Now it was looking bad.

The woman stood. "Colonel, do you mind if I take a few of your men back to the border to look around? Our contact may be trying to cross this afternoon."

Calvert really thought that it was useless, but he envied the lady's optimism. She hadn't been working in this godforsaken part of the world for enough years to know that things rarely went as planned. This was a part of the world that God obviously paid no attention to.

"Of course not. My men are at your disposal. I pray you will have some luck and find the notification we need to proceed. Believe me, the success of this mission is as important to me as it is to you."

"Not quite, Colonel," said the woman. She thought for a moment in silence and gave the officer an appreciative smile. "No... I really don't think so."

Marveling at her inner strength, Colonel Calvert remained in his chair as she turned and walked briskly out of his office. He suddenly wondered if she found him attractive, then mentally kicked himself for the thought. He was dealing with that exceptional woman on a professional basis. They were collaborating on an assignment. He must not allow himself to notice how well her uniform fit... or think about how he could console her when she finally realized that her people were lost.

21

The dining room had been turned into a conference hall. The huge table had been stripped of all ornaments and was completely bare. The place now looked like a typical corporate boardroom in which the powers that be meet to decide the future and direction of their organization. In a way, that was exactly what was going to happen that evening on the premises of General Tai Ta Chien.

The members of the cartel began to gather on the morning of the SOBs' fifth day of service to Chien. They came from all the dark corners of the Southeast Asian underworld. Most of them arrived by helicopter. They were greeted by Chien's servants upon their arrival and ushered to a common room for a formal welcome and refreshments. Each had his own room in the mansion and most would be staying the full three days to conduct their business.

Barrabas knew the strike had to take place imminently for it to have a maximum effect. Throughout his fifth day on the estate, he watched for Nanos and the strike force. He was on the lookout for some sign that they were near...that preparations were being made for the hit...that they might be waiting for a signal from Barrabas to make their move. All day there was nothing.

Barrabas and Diana watched from their room as the cartel members made their appearances, but the two crusaders stayed out of sight. They knew that if Nanos didn't make it back that day, they would have to be presented to the cartel at the evening meeting. Chien wanted to show off his new enforcement team. He had declared that the evening would be very entertaining and full of surprises.

Barrabas had no doubt that Chien was correct.

All the wrong elements were coming together. By late afternoon, Barrabas knew they were in trouble. They had no choice but to play out the charade. They couldn't run. Barrabas and his men could make their break when they were sent out in a day or so on another pointless mission for Chien.

But there was still Diana to think about. Barrabas still didn't know how he would get her out, and he couldn't leave her behind. The woman was Chien's ace in the hole.

Barrabas had one plan. He thought that Diana could become ill and have to be taken to a hospital or medical station. Then he learned that Chien had his own medic at the estate and one section of a team house was a complete field hospital. The idea went down the tube in a hurry.

The day was growing short, and there still was absolutely no sign of Nanos. Even allowing some margin for error and the unforeseen trouble that always popped up in the course of a mission, the Greek SOB should have made it to Nepal by midday and back with the strike force before nightfall.

They would not attack after dark. Barrabas knew Nanos was good, but he doubted that even the Greek Coast Guard vet could locate the estate after dark. He would need his markers, the signs he had set during his trip west. Nanos could determine direction after sundown with the best of them, but the Kumon Range and wild terrain of northern Burma would be impossible at night. The estate would be lit, but more was needed... some type of flare or signal from within. Something that Barrabas just couldn't provide.

Barrabas noted that Billy and Hayes were becoming restless. They wandered the grounds, spending an unusual amount of time in the yard. Barrabas knew that his two comrades were watching for Nanos... praying for the strike to begin.

All day there was nothing.

As night began to envelop them, Barrabas and Diana knew they were going to have to make an appearance before the cartel. But Barrabas couldn't shake his concern about Nanos. Losing a good man like the Greek was unthinkable! He had to force himself to concentrate on the problem at hand. He and the DEA agent were about to be presented before the warlords of Chien's drug cartel. They were powerful, evil men who hated the woman known as the Dragon Lady with a passion. Barrabas was aware that the toughest part of it would be convincing those guys not to kill her.

Barrabas stood in front of the huge closet and looked at the clothes. No use letting panic reign. He saw that Diana was glumly taking out a dress. It was clear that panic was about to beset her.

"We should just wear what we want to die in!" she said, throwing the gown to the floor.

A few moments later, Po was at the door, ready to escort them into the meeting room. They left the safety of their room and followed the servant down the long hallway. Diana felt like bawling. Now she knew how the last walk down death row felt. She decided that if she got out of this with her life, she would do everything in her power to stop capital punishment. She would also think a lot more seriously about that job as a schoolteacher.

Inside the dining hall, six of the seven warlords had gathered around the table. Chief Wa Duc was the only missing member of the cartel. Chien had decided to proceed without the Wa chief. Messengers sent to the chief's land had assured the general that the chief was on his way to the estate, but Chien didn't want to hold up the meeting. He was a man who respected schedules.

General Tai Ta Chien sat at the head of the table, in the place where he had taken supper with Barrabas and Diana on their first night at the estate. It was obviously the seat of honor, where the man in charge sat. There were no doubts that Chien was the man in charge. The other five drug kingpins were arguing among themselves, engaging in petty squabbles about opium shipments, land rights and women. Then Chien spoke, and all quarrels stopped. The five turned to face the general and waited for him to commence speaking.

"We have much business to discuss over the next few days. We shall proceed in a professional manner. Our primary concern this evening shall be the arms shipments we are receiving from Vietnam.

"Before we begin the true business of the evening, I have some information to share with you. First I must tell you the unfortunate news that our enforcement officer, Captain Marshall Edmond, is no longer with us. He was killed in the line of duty."

Colonel Van Minh Tho of the New Mon State Party was sitting on Chien's left. When he heard the news he began clapping. "Good! That is good! Captain Edmond was a pig!"

General Chien shrugged nonchalantly. "He served his purpose. I can report to you that his vacancy has been filled . . . by the man who killed him in fact. Colonel Nile Barrabas, formerly of the V.S. Army Special Forces, is now our officer in charge of enforcement policies."

Chien turned and nodded at Po, who was standing just inside the door of the dining room, waiting for the signal. He bowed to his leader, opened the door and spoke to someone in the hall, and Barrabas and Diana entered the room.

Diana's legs felt weak and wobbly. She walked a short way into the huge room and stopped. She stood as straight as she could, facing the table where six of her worst enemies sat looking at her, and tried to look cool. She thought about how nice it was going to be walking into a classroom full of children in the morning. . . .

Barrabas entered the dining hall and walked right up to stand next to General Chien. He faced the table with a solemn look. "Gentlemen, we meet again," he said, and there was an insolent tone in his voice that Chien immediately detected.

"Barrabas," said Chien, holding his hand up in front of the merc leader, "you will speak with respect to this group, or you will say nothing!"

Barrabas stopped talking.

General Than Hyut Linh of the Karen Unity Forces virtually jumped out of his chair as if jolted by an electric shock. He was the man who had tried to have Barrabas executed in Rangoon. He pointed at Barrabas, his hand shaking, and started sputtering. "Agh! Now is our chance! Kill him! He was supposed to be dead! He must be taken out."

Chien spoke soothingly to General Linh. "That is true. Unfortunately Captain Edmond and his men failed in the task. To our luck, Colonel Barrabas was available to replace the unfortunate captain."

Master Vien Quot, a Laotian land baron, was pointing at Diana. "You have not brought us luck, General Chien. You have placed a curse on us. That is the Dragon Lady, the woman who has been hunting us!"

Chien continued to speak in a soft, calm manner. "She is no longer with the DEA. She has seen the error of her ways and has decided to join us and seek her fortune. She is Colonel Barrabas's partner. Full partner—they take a lot of showers together," he added by way of clarification, emphasizing the words.

Diana blushed. Despite the fact that her stomach was in knots and she knew she was going to die, she felt embarrassed about the intimacy with Barrabas.

But she stood tall, saying nothing. She thought it best to let General Chien do the talking. She tried to smile at the warlords, and hoped she wasn't looking silly.

Master Quot couldn't be soothed. "This is not good! How can we trust this woman? You have brought our doom, General Chien! We are doomed!"

General Linh was still standing. His chair had tipped over and fallen behind him. He kept pointing at Barrabas and repeating, "We must kill him!"

Pandemonium was taking over the meeting. The other warlords started to join in the protests. Colonel Tho pounded his fist on the table. General Linh refused to sit down.

General Chien just sighed and sat back in his chair. He decided to let them vent their anger for a while. Barrabas and Diana remained silent, taking the abuse calmly.

Chien was about to speak again, to bring the meeting back to order, when there was another disturbance. But it seemed to come from the hallway outside the room.

Po opened the door to see what was happening. He was instantly shoved back into the room by a Wa warrior. The native stepped into the room and stood with folded arms, ushering in his leader. Chief Wa Duc had arrived at last.

The Wa chieftain paraded into the meeting room in grand style. He walked over to the table and stood by his appointed seat, then remained standing in silence until the room was quiet and all eyes were on him. He laughed and began speaking in a jovial manner. "Greetings to you, my fellow lords. I have come at last . . . bearing a gift!"

Chien sat glaring at Wa Duc. "You are late. You are an insult to our organization."

Chief Wa Duc laughed again. "But what I have with me will make up for my tardiness. One of my hunting parties brought back a treasure to our village a few days ago. Please let me show you what they found."

Wa Duc turned to his man at the door and the native made a signal toward the hallway. A grinning Captain Marshall Edmond walked into the room.

Edmond was fresh and rested from his stay at the Wa village. He bore almost no resemblance to the animal the Wa hunters had pulled out of the jungle. He was clean and energetic. He walked right up to Barrabas and looked him up and down.

"Hello, Barrabas. You seem to have seen a ghost."

Barrabas kept his cool. "Not a ghost, Edmond. Just a slimy little son of a bitch who got lucky."

"And your luck is gone, pal!" stated Edmond. "You're as good as dead!"

General Chien was taking it all in with acute interest. There was an anticipatory gleam in his eyes.

Diana was standing next to the Wa warrior. He was the only one in the room who was as serious as she was. All the others seemed to find the situation hilarious.

Barrabas and Edmond stood grinning a death grin at each other. General Chien and his six warlords were jolly in the anticipation of some dread event.

It was all a nightmare, and Diana's throat felt so constricted by fear that even if she had wanted to, she couldn't have cried.

22

The sounds of late-afternoon New York City traffic assaulted Walker Jessup's ears. The noise was a nagging reminder that people were starting to go home from work. Soon it would be time for dinner. Jessup frowned and hoped the meeting wasn't going to take too long.

Ducett, Jessup's assistant, opened the door to Jessup's inner office and ushered his boss's guest inside. Then he gave Jessup a nod and closed the door again. Ducett knew when he shouldn't ask questions about the business at hand. He also knew when it was best not to know too much...for his own good. All his senses told him that this was one of those times.

Jessup didn't stand. He kept his bulk firmly planted in the comfortable chair behind his massive desk and continued frowning.

The man walked up to stand in front of the desk. He had the same stone-cold emotionless features that Jessup remembered from Washington. His suit was, of course, gray. Jessup felt he was addressing a shadow.

"Hello, Dean."

The drug enforcement executive gave the large man his best smile. It wasn't much. "Jessup. Thanks for seeing me."

"Have a seat." Jessup indicated the chair in front of his desk with a slight wave of his hand, and Dean sat down. "So what brings you to New York?"

"That business in Burma. Do you know what's going on over there?"

Jessup shrugged his huge shoulders. It was an act that appeared to take a lot of effort. "My people are in the country. It's been less than two weeks. I expect to hear something soon. That's about it." He thought for a moment and added, "But I know there's nothing to worry about."

"I'm afraid there is," stated the drug agent. "I have rather disturbing reports from our agency. It appears that our agent in the field, Diana Simone, has gone over. She reported briefly to her office upon her return to Rangoon, then disappeared. Intel sources have informed our agency that she joined up with a drug mercenary and is working on the other side of the fence."

Jessup shrugged again. "The plan is working perfectly. The mercenary is obviously Barrabas. He and your girl have infiltrated the enemy. They are most likely in the process of locating their target, which is the cartel's stronghold, and your next report will most certainly be news of the cartel's destruction." Jessup chuckled. "Hell . . . Barrabas and his people are probably blowing the shit out of the place right now."

"But you haven't heard directly from them?"

"No, but there's nothing to worry about. Trust me. It's the norm for Barrabas to be out of communication while in the field. He may be in a place where communication is impossible...or where any type of contact with the outside would mean his death. He may have penetrated the enemy."

"Do you have a way to get in touch with them?" asked Dean.

"I doubt it," said Jessup. "What's the problem? I assure you that everything is fine. Your girl is working under cover. The reports of her going over mean the plan is working."

"That's what I'm afraid of."

"What?"

The drug enforcement executive sighed and sat back in his seat. He spoke very softly, as if what he was saying were causing him pain. It also showed on his features. He looked sad, the first emotion Jessup had seen on this man.

"We have to abort the mission. You must make contact with Barrabas and call him back."

"Excuse me?!"

"I'm afraid...there are problems...complications. I'll explain as much as I can to you...."

"That's a damned good idea!" Jessup's frown had turned to a scowl. He was no longer concerned with his supper.

"It appears the leader of the cartel is one General Tai Ta Chien, the only Chinese member of the group."

"As I remember from your files, that was a theory from the beginning," said Jessup. "And the cartel's stronghold could be located on his land in northern Burma."

"I don't know that for sure," said Dean. "It's certainly a possibility. I'm afraid it no longer matters. My new orders are to leave General Chien alone."

"Oh, for God's sake! He's a poppy general! One of the East's most notorious drug warlords!"

"That is all very true. He is also a devoted anti-Communist. The money he's making on his drug operations is going to support his plans to overthrow the Chinese government. His drug cartel is serving as a way to unite the Southeast Asian states and unify them for the first time in a common cause. The money they make on the sale of opium is used to buy arms and support their army. There are many people inside our government communities who honestly believe Chien's plan has a chance. They actually support his efforts...indirectly, of course. There is an agent in place...."

"Edmond!" Jessup was actually grinning from the insanity of it all.

"Yes, Captain Edmond is working for this agency."

"Ha! Edmond is working for the CIA! Barrabas is hunting him for the DEA! This is good!" Jessup sat back in his chair and chuckled. It was another classic example of the right hand not knowing what the left hand was doing. Jessup laughed harder. "It's so typical!"

Dean saw no humor in the situation. He continued to look very sad. "I'm glad you find it so funny, Jessup. My neck happens to be in a noose."

"I don't see why. Hell, you were only doing your job. Chien and his cartel are a menace. They currently operate the largest dealership of drugs in Southeast Asia. You had no idea they were being supported by the CIA."

"Only indirectly," stated Dean. "I don't want you to get the idea that a government agency is directly involved in the dealing of drugs."

"Heaven forbid!" said Jessup. He had been in this business for too many years to think that the players in the secret games had any morals. Those creatures decided on an objective and they didn't care what they did to reach it. One agency wanted to support Chien's plan to overthrow Red China. Another agency wanted to destroy Chien's drug operations. Now their agents were clashing in the field. He had seen it all before.

The agent looked really depressed. Jessup felt sorry for him and decided to help him out. "Look, Dean, swallow your pride, forget all about the code of ethics you guys live by and take this thing upstairs. The administration will support you. When it comes to a choice between putting a major drug operation out of business or supporting some wacko general's revolution, the drug bust wins every time. Look what happened in Panama."

"We don't like to take our business outside the community. There could be a scandal. There will certainly be a shake-up and subsequent investigations. We just don't need another mess right now."

"I don't think you have a choice," said Jessup.

"The easiest and best solution would be to call Barrabas back. Abort the mission. Let things smooth out over there. My people will back off and let the agency take it. We have enough other work to keep us busy.''

"You don't seem to understand the situation that you've created. That's Nile Barrabas you've sent over there. His mission is to destroy the cartel. He will not come back until he accomplishes his objective. Even if I could make contact with him, I doubt I could stop him. He's not one of your agency boys, all happy members of the community social club. He believes in what he's doing. He won't be stopped.''

Dean ceased looking sad and started looking physically ill. Jessup was his only chance to get out of the predicament smoothly. He would now have to go up to administration with the mess. Heads would roll. Network executives would be crucified. His only hope was that the man he would deal with hated drugs more than Communism.

23

He thought it was still morning. He opened his eyes and tried to understand what was happening. It didn't hurt as much after the second nap. His head throbbed dully, but at least it wasn't that stabbing pain he had experienced the first time he'd tried to come back to life.

He couldn't move his right arm. Someone had tied it down. Or was that a bandage? There was no pain, and he didn't remember having pain in the arm. It was numb. It was good that there was no pain, but it wasn't good that there was no feeling at all. All that blood didn't bode much good.

The sun was rising in front of them. It was coming up in the west. That wasn't right, unless they were going the wrong way! They were going back to Burma! Or maybe they were going to China! It just wasn't right.

He tried to sit up straight. The seat was narrow. There was no cab on the truck...it must have been torn off when they'd rolled. The bench seat was gone, too. And then he knew he wasn't in the truck. He was in a jeep.

He was going to China!

He made a noise and tried to fight. His left arm lashed out and flailed around a bit. He had no strength.

"No, no. Stop it, boss. It okay!"

The driver was speaking in broken English. Nanos turned his head painfully and tried to focus his vision. Mai Su was driving. Why was Mai Su driving them back to Burma?

"Wrong...Mai...you're wrong...."

"It okay, boss. Just rest."

Nanos did as he was told. He closed his eyes and the pain went away. It felt good just to lie in the seat and let the blackness back into his life. Take him.

But he had to think, and that ruined everything. Thinking hurt. He remembered fleeing the Chinese roadblock; the hit the truck took and Bo San's death; the rollover and the round in his arm and hitting his head and blackness. He tried to think of a reason to be heading back to Burma. He remembered opening his eyes before and finding Mai Su in charge, taking care of him...getting him into the jeep. He realized the Langtao warrior must have won the fight against the Chinese patrol. They were taking the jeep, and they were going on!

They had not turned back toward Burma. That was why the sun was in front of them...it was nightfall, not morning! They were heading west.

He remembered opening his eyes and finding the sun above them. The first time he came back to life it must have been midday. Mai Su had been struggling all day to get them to Nepal.

They were going on!

It wasn't over. They were driving west, over a day late... but they could still make it!

"Hey... Mai... let's go for it!"

"You rest. It okay. You just rest, boss."

"Hot damn! I live!"

"And I drive. You just rest now. It okay!"

Nanos grinned. He closed his eyes again and that felt good. In fact, it felt so good, he decided to keep his eyes shut for a while. The rocking and gentle bouncing of the jeep lulled him. The jeep had good shocks. He rested, and soon he was dozing again.

He knew they were in trouble in his sleep. He didn't know if it was a dream or reality. He didn't want to know that there was trouble... he just wanted peace and rest and a moving jeep.

But he had to know. He opened his eyes and saw the roadblock ahead. Mai Sui was slowing down. The dangerous silhouettes of armed soldiers were moving around in the twilight. Why was Mai Su driving up there?

"Turn... Mai... turn it... shit!"

Nanos made a weak grab for the steering wheel of the jeep. Mai Su pushed his arm away.

"It okay, boss! It okay!"

They were driving up to the roadblock. Where was his weapon? Nanos didn't want to give up now! They had to be close to Nepal!

He had no weapon. He had lost his M-16. Mai Su still had his gun, but he wasn't going to use it.

They drove up to the roadblock. A soldier stopped the jeep and walked up to speak with Mai Su. Nanos couldn't understand what they were saying. It wasn't Chinese.

Then there was another voice...a commanding voice that spoke over the two talking Asians. A female voice.

"Over here! Here! We found them!"

Nanos sat up in his seat. He tried to focus his eyes to see what this roadblock was all about.

He looked to his right and saw the woman approaching. She was dressed in a night-black combat uniform. She had a group of heavily armed soldiers with her. She was walking toward the jeep.

"Oh, great..."

It was probably some lady warlord looking for political clout. He would end up in some dungeon in Tibet or Mongolia, a tool in the never-ending war.

Mai Su was getting out of the jeep. Nanos called after him. "Mai—" When there was no response, he looked around.

It wasn't a roadblock! They were at the border. It was a border crossing.

They had reached Nepal!

"Hello, Alex."

The lady warlord spoke to him. She knew his name. He turned to her, focused his eyes and looked at her hard. "It's you! Son of a bitch!"

"No," said the lady. "Soldier of Barrabas."

Lee Hatton, the female SOB, put her arm around her comrade. "Help me," she said to the Gurkhas with her.

Together they lifted Nanos out of the jeep. He wore a weak and silly grin.

24

The late-morning sun was exceptionally hot as a crowd of more than a hundred men and women gathered in the courtyard of Chien's estate to watch a man die. The air was particularly thick and humid that day, but it did nothing to inhibit the enjoyment of the revelers.

Barrabas and Edmond stood in the center of the lawn, facing each other a yard apart. Their left arms had been tied by a three-foot cord. They both wore the same uniform of plain jungle fatigues. They had no belts, nothing in their pockets, and the only articles of clothing they could use as weapons were their boots. In their right hands they each held double-edged Legionnaire combat knives.

The seven warlords were sitting on chairs set up theater-style on the landscaped grounds, where the entertainment was about to take place. Chien's servants were preparing brunch on the patio behind them. It promised to be a morning of fun and sport before the business of the cartel commenced in the afternoon.

Diana, Billy and Hayes stood next to the seated warlords. Xonn, the Tibetan bodyguard, watched them. He still brandished his K-38 submachine gun. If one of them attempted to intervene in the game, Xonn's orders were to kill him.

Billy Two and Hayes had had their weapons taken from them. They and the Dragon Lady were now to become the spoils for the winner of the competition. The winner would have the enforcement team to do with as he pleased. Edmond had already announced that he would execute them and put together his own team. He would slit the SOBs' throats. As for the female agent, she would share the same fate after he'd had a few days of her.

Marshall Edmond's face was fixed in an insane-looking smile. This was the moment he had survived in the jungles for... his time of glorious revenge! The death he gave Barrabas would be a celebration!

Nile Barrabas had dropped his guise. He was no longer grinning, no longer flippant. His features were stern. He was again the cold, calculating soldier of a dozen wars. His mind was working on a plan to save his people... to escape. They were on their own, weaponless except for the knife he held, and he was tied to a man whose sole ambition was to kill him.

Barrabas was still forming a plan, when Chien got up from his chair and spoke. As the Chinese general lifted an arm and began to talk, a hush fell over the crowd of observers.

"It is time for a decision to be made by skill. One of these men shall serve as our enforcer. The man who survives the test will have proven that he is best suited for the position."

The jungle lowlife laughed, and last-minute bets were placed in haste. The crowd moved in around the two combatants, anticipation spreading.

Colonel Tho leaned in his chair and spoke softly to General Linh. "Who is the favorite?"

The Burmese general gave a slight shrug. "I believe it is Captain Edmond…not so much for his skills, but because many of the men would like to see Barrabas killed and his men's throats cut."

Colonel Tho smiled and nodded. "Yes, that would be good."

General Chien continued with his speech. "Of course, if both men are killed, we will be forced to find another for the job. It is a dilemma I am willing to face for the sake of our entertainment. So, it is time to begin the game. As the saying goes, may the best man win! You may start."

Chien sat down. But before he was completely seated, Edmond made a lunge at Barrabas.

Barrabas jumped aside, narrowly dodging the thrust. He pulled as hard as he could on the cord that tied their arms and brought his right arm above his head. With a mighty sweep he used all his strength and broke the cord in two. Edmond whirled and prepared for a second lunge. Barrabas blocked the attack with a sidesweep of his left arm, and finally free, he jumped back, putting a safe distance between Edmond and himself.

Marshall Edmond was hungry for blood. The jungle animal had awakened in him again. He would kill to survive! Kill for revenge! He turned on Barrabas and brought his knife up for another strike.

Barrabas braced himself, ready for the next assault. He watched his opponent's eyes and listened to the noise of the crowd around him. Over the uproar of the cheering and jeering spectators, he heard a lone voice. A man on guard duty in one of the perimeter towers was yelling something. A warning. But no one was paying any attention. All interest was on the duel-to-the-death going on in the center of the yard.

Edmond lunged again. Barrabas jumped aside, blocked and felt the blade cut into the flesh of his forearm. Edmond had been expecting his move that time. Barrabas wasn't concentrating on the fight, but on the whup...whup...whup...coming over the western horizon.

More guards were yelling, but Edmond's ferocious scream drowned out their shouts of panic as he charged at Barrabas. The mercenary colonel waved his knife, distracting Edmond's vision, then put everything he had into a left roundhouse that caught the ex-captain on the right cheek. Edmond's scream was now one of pure pain, and Barrabas felt something splinter as he followed through on the punch and leaped over Edmond's falling body, diving straight at the warlords.

"Billy...Hayes...cover me!"

Xonn saw Barrabas going for his masters. He lifted the SMG to defend them, and both SOBs hit him at once. His huge body dropped to the ground, and Hayes went for the weapon. He grabbed it, spun around on one knee to fire, and the crowd of jungle criminals and drug soldiers was hit from two directions at once: from the front as the deadly spray of the

DSh K-38 cut into them, and from above as five British assault choppers swept out of the hills and came down with a precise and controlled fury. Mounted M-60s spit death, and dragons erupted to fire streaking thunder onto the estate. Team houses erupted in flame. A guard tower took a direct hit and burning, shrieking men plunged to the ground.

As the strike force made its initial hit, Barrabas dove in among the warlords. They screamed in total panic, fell off their seats, rolled, tried desperately to get out of the path of the crazed mercenary colonel. Barrabas hit them in a rolling block, grabbed at uniforms, robes, soft flesh. He felt his fingers dig into a face and felt the warm flow of gushing blood followed by an ear-piercing shriek of pain.

He continued rolling, over and away from the floundering group of poppy kingpins. His plan was to plunge them into a total state of chaos so there would be no leadership to defend the estate against the attack.

His plan worked. The drug warlords cared only about saving themselves. They crawled away, stood and made for the house in haste as the choppers turned and descended and Gurkha commandos began to leap out and drop down onto the lawn. They became engaged in close combat with the army of drug soldiers.

Barrabas had disengaged himself and he looked around to get a quick fix on the situation. All hell had broken loose, but it appeared things were still going in the striker's favor.

Billy now had a weapon, an M-1 with a full clip. He was beside Diana, grinning at Barrabas. He gave his leader a salute and turned to join in the fight. Diana stood perfectly still at his side, a look of absolute terror on her face. She was caught right in the heart of a full combat situation, and she was petrified. To Barrabas she had proven herself, and he knew she would be all right with Billy. He turned his attention to another matter.

The lead attack vehicle, a Royal Air Force Wessex combat helicopter, was landing in the courtyard where Barrabas had been facing off with Edmond a few moments ago. The chopper came to a smooth, easy landing—the pilot apparently very familiar with combat situations—and the troops inside began leaping out.

First came Colonel Jonathan Calvert in full battle dress. He scanned the field of battle around him and took a quick check of the situation. He was happy with what he saw. His force was doing an excellent job.

Behind the colonel, Lee Hatton jumped from the chopper. After her came a worn, disheveled Alex Nanos, his head wrapped with a bandage and his right arm in a sling. It appeared to Barrabas that his man had had a bit of trouble on the trip to Nepal. But he had made it, and it was the final result that counted. And even though he looked weary and wounded, there was the fire of battle in Nanos's eyes and a grin of determination on his hard features. He was ready for a fight.

Directly behind Nanos, Mai Su lunged out of the chopper, a huge grin on his face and his prized M-1 carbine in his relentless grip. He had seen the mission to its finale. Barrabas watched him with pride as the Langtao warrior joined the battle.

Barrabas stepped down from the patio and waved to his people. Calvert saw him and returned the wave. Then he, Nanos, Lee and Mai Su ran toward Barrabas.

Behind them, the rest of the helicopters had landed on the estate grounds, and the Gurkha strike force was completely engaged with the drug army. The bandits and opium mercenaries were no match for the highly trained professionals. The Gurkha force was cutting down all resistance with well-aimed fire and close-quarter combat. The team houses were ablaze as the strikers lobbed grenades into them, then cut down the men who dashed outside. The defending drug soldiers were falling in droves with shouts of defeat and curses. The Gurkhas were showing no mercy.

Colonel Calvert approached Barrabas and held out his hand. They shook and greeted each other as old friends.

"Colonel Nile Barrabas . . . only you could find this place out here in the middle of hell. I can't believe you and your people actually pulled this thing off. You have a very determined team, Colonel."

"They're good people," said Barrabas, looking over the British soldier's shoulder and giving Nanos a little nod. "Have some trouble, Alex?"

"A few minor diversions, Colonel." The Greek SOB gave his leader a little smile and shrugged. "It was a piece of cake, really."

"So it seems," stated Barrabas, eyeing Nanos. He looked terrible.

Calvert was watching the battle on the estate. "We're cleaning up a lot of old business here. There are more wanted criminals and bandits and drug dealers out there than in all the prisons in Indochina."

"The really big fish are inside the house, Colonel," said Barrabas. "All the members of the cartel, including General Chien."

"Nanos tells me this is Chien's property," said Calvert.

"That's right. And he's the leader of the cartel. The other warlords all take orders from him."

"Well, I suggest we go in and make this mission a complete success." Calvert gave the battle a last look. "Things appear to be in order out there."

Claude Hayes, accompanied by two Gurkha strikers, ran over to assist them. Hayes gave Nanos a hard look and then a big grin. "You look like shit, Alex!"

"Well, crap! I didn't have the easy end of it like you guys back here in the lap of luxury!"

"Yeah . . . and you took your goddam time about getting back—"

"Enough of that," Barrabas told his men. "Are you ready to finish this thing off, Colonel?" he asked Calvert.

"Ready, Colonel!"

"Let's do it!"

The assault team turned to face the mansion. Reflections of burning team houses and fire from the erupting battle shone from the front of the big house. The thunder of war enveloped the entire estate.

Out of the orange glow stepped Po. He stood at the entrance to the mansion, the final guardian, holding an M-1 clumsily in his shaking hands. He was not a warrior, he was a servant, but he was going to defend his master's property to the end.

Barrabas felt a certain pride for the loyal man. "Put the weapon down, Po. There's no need to die."

Po looked as sad as a human being is capable of as he lifted the rifle and tried to shoot Barrabas. Hayes, Nanos, Lee Hatton and the two Gurkhas fired simultaneously on the hapless man. His body was torn apart by the barrage and flipped back through the open doorway. He was dead before he hit the floor.

Barrabas and the assault team stood in silence for a moment, the shots still ringing inside their heads, almost drowning out the other sounds of battle behind them. They stared at the carnage they had created, a bit stunned.

"That guy was crazy," Hayes said, as if speaking for more than himself.

"Just doing his job," said Barrabas. "Like us. Let's go."

He led the team through the front entrance of the mansion. They went through the doorway cautiously, stepping over Po's mangled body and moving with care into the foyer. They met no further resistance.

The team fanned out and moved through the huge mansion, searching for the seven warlords. Barrabas ordered the soldiers to spread out, but was certain he knew where Chien and the others were waiting. He motioned Colonel Calvert to accompany him.

Barrabas led Calvert down the main hall and into the dining room. There were the seven warlords, seated at the table. Six of them, all except Chien, who sat calmly at his place at the head of the table, were dead.

Chien's two servant girls stood on each side of him, still clutching the smoking AK-47s. Barrabas knew the scenario. Chien had brought the cartel together in the dining hall, telling them they needed a fast meeting before fleeing into the jungles. He knew it was over. He sat the six kingpins at the table, three on each side, and the two girls entered behind them and shot them through the head. If the Chinese general's dreams were finished, they were to be completely finished. It was the ending.

Barrabas and Calvert stood at the opposite end of the table, staring at Chien in silence for a long moment. The girls did not raise their weapons in defense.

Finally Calvert spoke. "General Tai Ta Chien, I arrest you in the name of the British government for crimes committed within her realm and against humanity."

Chien smiled. "You will not arrest me, Colonel. I invite you to sit with me and share the ending of my dreams."

Barrabas suddenly understood what was happening. "Colonel—get the team outside! Quickly! This place is laced with plastic explosives. It's going up any minute!"

Calvert didn't need to be told twice. He nodded at Barrabas and ran from the room. Barrabas stood in his place and continued to face Chien.

"You have chosen to die with me?" asked the Chinese general.

"Not a chance. I want you to know in no uncertain terms that if you try to escape, I will kill you."

Chien continued to smile. "A man such as you, Colonel Barrabas, must certainly have shared in my dream."

"Your philosophy was right, Chien, but your methods were grossly wrong."

"Ah! So you are not the mercenary I thought. You are a crusader with a big heart."

"I'm just a man who doesn't like to see kids dying from your drugs. You had to be stopped."

"And you have succeeded." Chien gave Barrabas a formal bow. "I commend you. But for your efforts, you must now pay the ultimate price."

Xonn, the huge Tibetan, had stepped into the dining room behind Barrabas. As Chien made his final threat, Barrabas turned to bolt, and was instantly clutched by the bodyguard in a bear hug from behind.

Xonn held Barrabas in the room. The explosives were obviously going to blow at any moment. They would all die together!

Barrabas struggled, pushing, kicking, trying to batter the Tibetan's face with the back of his head. He could not break the incredibly strong grip of the loyal bodyguard.

"Goodbye, Colonel Barrabas," said Chien. "We will no doubt meet again in the place of our ancestors."

Barrabas lifted his legs and pushed on the edge of the massive table with all his remaining strength. The Tibetan staggered back a few steps but held tight. Barrabas could not break his grip.

Chien sat calmly at the head of the table. He looked at his two girls and took their hands in his. One of them gave a quiet sob. They stood by their master and braced themselves to die.

Barrabas heaved against Xonn's grip. There was a sudden shudder and an explosion that drowned out the sound of the shot from the doorway. The first bomb was going off somewhere upstairs. It was followed by a closer rumble, and Xonn, already dead, let go of Barrabas.

Barrabas lurched forward, suddenly free. He turned and saw that the back of Xonn's head was blown off. Colonel Calvert stood in the doorway, his rifle still raised in the position he had used to shoot the bodyguard.

"Kill him! Kill Barrabas!"

On Chien's desperate command, the two girls lifted their AKs. Calvert shifted and shot the servant on the left.

Barrabas grabbed one of the chairs from the dining set. Burning debris was falling into the room. Another explosion took out the south wing. Paintings were dropping off the walls. Lamps and ornaments were crashing on the floor. Barrabas swung around and heaved the chair through the window on his right.

Calvert was aiming at the other girl while she tried to decide whether she should shoot him or Barrabas.

"Jon! Never mind that! Get the hell out!" Barrabas reached out and pulled the British colonel toward the gaping window.

Chien stood and pointed at them. "Kill them! Kill both of them!"

The female servant was shaking with sobs. She brought the AK around as Barrabas and Calvert leaped through the window and the dining hall exploded.

Outside, Hayes, Nanos and Lee stood in a little group and watched the entire house erupt in one gigantic ball of flame. They knew that the colonel was still inside.

"No!" Lee Hatton gasped when she was the final explosion. One hand went to her mouth.

"Damn!" Hayes pointed at the inferno as two shadows surrounded by flames appeared, then flew out of the fire. Barrabas and Calvert hit the ground and rolled. The entire mansion exploded above them. They clutched at the ground as a wave of heat and flame swept inches above them.

Barrabas and Calvert lurched to their feet and dashed away from the incredible inferno behind them. The SOBs ran over to meet them. The two colonels looked a bit singed, but for the most part were unharmed.

They all turned for a moment to watch the burning mansion with a kind of awe. Flames and billowing black smoke obscured the jungle skies.

Barrabas turned to his left and looked hard at Calvert. "Are you out of your mind? You must be completely nuts to have gone back in there!"

Calvert gave the other colonel a stern look. "You should talk, Barrabas! You picked a ruddy bloody bad time to dance with that ugly bloke!"

Barrabas was about to chastise his British friend some more for doing something so stupid, when he was distracted by somebody calling his name.

"Colonel Barrabas!"

A Gurkha soldier was approaching, clutching at a wounded man. It was Billy!

Barrabas stepped over to them. He placed an arm around Billy. "What happened?"

Billy looked up at him and spoke with effort. He had been knifed deeply in the side and was bleeding profusely. "It was Edmond. He caught me from behind. He got away, Colonel . . . went into the jungle."

"Which way?" asked Barrabas.

Billy pointed north. Barrabas turned him over to the Gurkha soldier to tend to his wound. Billy was cut badly and needed medical attention, but he would be okay. He had suffered much worse.

Barrabas turned to let Calvert know the situation, when Billy called to him again. "Colonel . . . he . . . he took Diana!"

25

The battle was over. The strike force had won. The Gurkhas were rounding up the remainder of the drug soldiers. All the fight was gone out of the little army.

The estate was burning steadily. The warlords were all dead. Nile Barrabas had let the British colonel tend to the details of wrapping up the operation.

He headed north.

Barrabas had one more job to finish before his mission was completed.

It was a job that had started fifteen years ago on the streets of Saigon....

CLAUDE HAYES, Alex Nanos and Lee Hatton stood in a group looking past one of the smoldering team houses into the dense jungles. Colonel Jonathan Calvert spotted them and walked over to stand next to Hatton. The SOBs looked tired and pensive. The past two weeks in Southeast Asia had not been a vacation for them.

"That about wraps it up here," said Calvert. "We've closed a lot of old business today. The opium trade in Indochina and the Orient will be in turmoil for a while. I still can't believe you chaps actually pulled this thing off."

Nanos shrugged, his right arm still resting in the sling. "Just another job for us. I'm ready to start the next one."

"Oh, man!" Hayes gave Nanos a sincere look of disgust. "Give us a break! You're so full of shit it's running out your mouth!"

Calvert laughed. "You all look like the devil's had you for breakfast. I believe you are due some R and R. If I were Barrabas, I'd see to it each of you was rewarded justly. By the way, where is Colonel Barrabas?"

"He went into the bush," said Lee Hatton. "He has some unfinished business."

"That damned fool!" said Calvert, looking concerned. "He went out after Edmond! Alone! Why couldn't he wait?"

"It's just something he has to do, Colonel," said Hatton. "He has to take care of it his way. It's become a personal thing."

Calvert nodded with understanding. "Bloody hero! He reminds me of myself."

Lee Hatton turned slightly and gave Calvert a captivating smile. "There are certain similarities."

The British colonel's heart missed a beat. The woman was even gorgeous right after combat!

THE JUNGLE NORTH of Chien's estate was thick and dense. The only trail leading through the foliage was the one Edmond had made dragging Diana. It was easy to follow.

Barrabas pushed through the brush, moving quickly but carefully. The knife cut on his left forearm had started to bleed again; red streamed from the tips of his fingers. Barrabas ignored the pain.

He came into a small, grassy clearing. He knew he would find Edmond there. His instincts told him this would be the final place.

"Hello, Barrabas. Nice of you to come."

Barrabas turned to his right. Standing near the edge of the clearing were Edmond and Diana. The merc captain stood behind the girl, clutching her, his Legionnaire knife at her throat. One motion, and he could end her life in a most brutal fashion.

"Let her go, Edmond."

"In a moment, buddy. I just want to be sure you know the rules of our game."

"I can imagine."

Edmond laughed softly. "It had to come to this, didn't it? I mean, ever since Saigon, I've known that we would be here someday. And it's really kind of funny...."

"What's funny?" asked Barrabas.

"We're really both on the same side."

Barrabas nodded. He had thought so. "You're CIA."

"More or less," said Edmond, laughing again. "And you're DEA."

"Something like that."

Edmond was still laughing. "This is rich. Two covert ops of the Special Warfare communities, assigned to work against each other."

"I don't suppose you would go back with me?" suggested Barrabas. "It doesn't really have to come to this. You'll be arrested...."

"Not a chance, Barrabas. I'd never give up without a fight—you know that. And I have to kill you."

Barrabas nodded again. He had known the answer. "I can't let you get away with your crimes, Edmond. I don't care who you were working for or where your orders came from. You operated an illegal death squad. You have committed thousands of murders, directly and indirectly, through your drug dealings. You are a completely amoral man. Nothing, no cause, no sanction, can excuse you. You are a disgrace to the Special Forces."

"Shut up, Barrabas. Come here and take the girl."

Barrabas knew it was a ruse, but he had to get Diana to safety before he could act against Edmond. He took a step toward them and reached cautiously for the girl. "Step away from him, Diana. Come to me."

"Nile!"

She gave off one soft cry and Edmond pushed her head away, and she stumbled and fell on the ground to the left. Barrabas was open and an easy target as Edmond thrust with the combat knife, going for the throat.

That was his mistake. He was too eager to kill. He should have gone for the torso, a larger target that would have taken Barrabas longer to move from harm's way.

Barrabas dodged the knife, felt Edmond's arm glance off his shoulder and go past. He ducked and prepared to counterthrust with his own Legionnaire, but Edmond followed through correctly and danced past Barrabas. They both turned simultaneously, close together, and lashed out with their free hands to grab the other's fatigue shirt. They clutched the fabric and held. They would not part until it was over.

Edmond swiped at Barrabas, hoping for a lethal cut. Barrabas blocked it. Edmond tried again quickly, hoping to catch Barrabas off guard. It didn't work; Barrabas blocked once more.

Barrabas twisted the material of Edmond's shirt, holding him close. Barrabas's arm was bleeding profusely and the pain was worse, but he was still able to block it from his mind. He concentrated on the fight, on survival.

Edmond's face was discolored where Barrabas had caught him with the punch. One eye was swelling shut. Barrabas tried to knee Edmond in the groin, but he turned his strong body and easily blocked the move. Then Edmond made the first mistake. His concentration faltered and he looked into Barrabas's eyes, and he saw something, the thing that would not be beaten, the soul of the man he was fighting. And Edmond was frightened.

Captain Marshall Edmond took one small step backward. It was all Barrabas needed. He butted his head into Edmond's broken face and felt bone smash. Edmond screamed, and Barrabas shifted his strength and weight and pushed. Edmond tripped on a patch of broken sod and lost his footing, and he knew he was going to die.

"No!"

Edmond started to go down. Barrabas had him and knew Edmond would not be able to strike effectively again. He pushed and held him down, waiting for submission.

If Edmond had given in to Barrabas, admitted defeat or asked for his life, he would have survived. His instincts told him the fight was over; something told him to live. But the animal got the best of him again. He turned on his elbow and threw the knife at the semiprone woman who was watching fearfully.

"No!"

"No!"

Both men yelled the word at the same time. No, the other would not win! But the knife missed the woman's face by an inch, and Barrabas thrust straight and clean with his Legionnaire and buried it into Captain Marshall Edmond's chest.

Barrabas was frozen. Blood pumped on him, spraying from the wound in the dead man's chest. He shook slightly, using his strength to push the knife deeper. He still clutched Edmond's shirt and his fingernails were torn and bleeding with the effort.

"No...no...no..."

"It's over, Nile. Let him go. It's over."

Diana was gently pulling on Barrabas. He felt her gentleness and he relaxed. He let go of the knife, and the stress left his body as he stood. He turned toward her, and saw that the tears had made streaks on her face. She looked a bit silly, like a sad clown in the circus.

Barrabas held her. He spoke softly into her hair. "It's okay...yes...it's all over. We made it."

Colonel Calvert, Lee Hatton, Alex Nanos and Claude Hayes stepped into the clearing and walked over to them. Barrabas was comforting Diana, gently soothing her over the lifeless body of Marshall Edmond, whose blood still flowed into the Burmese soil.

The British colonel and SOBs stood quietly behind them for a moment. The only sounds were Diana's tiny sobs of relief.

Nanos spoke first. "Are you all right, Colonel?"

"Yes, Alex. Fine."

"Orders?"

Barrabas looked over Diana's shoulder. The complete weariness in his eyes touched the others. "Yes. Let's get out of here."

Barrabas released his hold on Diana. She looked at him and wanted to say something, but the words caught in her throat.

Before he started to lead them from the clearing, Barrabas said, "And just remember, we'll have to fill in O'Toole. He'll need the material for that epic poem." The white-haired mercenary's statement was followed by a chorus of dismayed groans.

"Gar Wilson is excellent. Raw action attacks the reader from every page."
—Don Pendleton

SUPER PHOENIX FORCE #1
FIRE STORM

An international peace conference turns into open warfare when terrorists kidnap the American President and the premier of the USSR at a summit meeting. As a last desperate measure, Phoenix Force is brought in—for if demands are not met, a plutonium core device is set to explode.

Available in November at your favorite retail outlet, or reserve your copy for October shipping by sending your name, address, zip or postal code along with a check or money order for $4.70 (includes 75¢ for postage and handling) payable to Gold Eagle Books:

In the U.S.	In Canada
Gold Eagle Books	Gold Eagle Books
901 Fuhrmann Blvd.	P.O. Box 609
Box 1325	Fort Erie, Ontario
Buffalo, NY 14269-1325	L2A 5X3

Please specify book title with your order.

GOLD EAGLE

SPF-1

DON PENDLETON's
MACK BOLAN.

More SuperBolan bestseller action! Longer than the monthly series, SuperBolans feature Mack in more intricate, action-packed plots— more of a good thing

		Quantity
STONY MAN DOCTRINE follows the action of paramilitary strike squads, Phoenix Force and Able Team.	$3.95	☐
TERMINAL VELOCITY places Bolan in a KGB trap when the CIA has orders to kill him.	$2.95	☐
RESURRECTION DAY renews a long-standing war against the Mafia.	$3.95	☐
DIRTY WAR follows the group on a secret mission into Cambodia.	$3.95	☐
FLIGHT 741 forces Bolan into the role of hostage as radicals leave a path of death and destruction.	$3.95	☐
DEAD EASY tracks down an elusive but deadly Mafia-KGB connection.	$3.95	☐

Total Amount	$	
Plus 75¢ Postage		.75
Payment enclosed		

Please send a check or money order payable to Gold Eagle Books.

In the U.S.A.	In Canada	SMB-2
Gold Eagle Books	Gold Eagle Books	
901 Fuhrmann Blvd.	P.O. Box 609	
Box 1325	Fort Erie, Ontario	
Buffalo, NY 14269-1325	L2A 5X3	

Please Print

Name: _____

Address: _____

City: _____

State/Prov: _____

Zip/Postal Code: _____

TAKE 'EM NOW

FOLDING SUNGLASSES
FROM GOLD EAGLE

Mean up your act with these tough, street-smart shades. Practical, too, because they fold 3 times into a handy, zip-up polyurethane pouch that fits neatly into your pocket. Rugged metal frame. Scratch-resistant acrylic lenses. Best of all, they can be yours for only $6.99.

MAIL YOUR ORDER TODAY.

Send your name, address, and zip code, along with a check or money order for just $6.99 + .75¢ for postage and handling (for a total of $7.74) payable to Gold Eagle Reader Service. (New York and Iowa residents please add applicable sales tax.)

Remove from pouch...

unfold once...

GOLD EAGLE
Gold Eagle Reader Service
901 Fuhrmann Blvd.
P.O. Box 1396
Buffalo, N.Y. 14240-1396

unfold twice...

and they're ready to wear.

GES-1A

Offer not available in Canada.